BY JOHN McPHEE

SILK PARACHUTE

SILK PARACHUTE

JOHN McPHEE

FARRAR, STRAUS AND GIROUX

NEW YORK

Farrar, Straus and Giroux
18 West 18th Street, New York 10011

Copyright © 2010 by John McPhee
All rights reserved
Distributed in Canada by D&M Publishers, Inc.
Printed in the United States of America
First edition, 2010

Library of Congress Cataloging-in-Publication Data
McPhee, John, 1931–
   Silk parachute / John McPhee. — 1st ed.
      p.   cm.
   ISBN 978-0-374-26373-7
   1. McPhee, John, 1931– —Childhood and youth.   2. Authors, American—
20th century—Biography.   3. American essays.   I. Title.

AC8.M268 2010
810.9'005—dc22

                                                        2009031887

Designed by Abby Kagan

www.fsgbooks.com

1   3   5   7   9   10   8   6   4   2

FOR MY GRANDCHILDREN

ISOBEL

JASPER

LEANDRO

LIVIA

NICHOLAS

OLIVER

REBECCA

RILEY

TOMMASO

CONTENTS

SILK PARACHUTE

When your mother is ninety-nine years old, you have so many memories of her that they tend to overlap, intermingle, and blur. It is extremely difficult to single out one or two, impossible to remember any that exemplify the whole.

It has been alleged that when I was in college she heard that I had stayed up all night playing poker and wrote me a letter that used the word "shame" forty-two times. I do not recall this.

I do not recall being pulled out of my college room and into the church next door.

It has been alleged that on December 24, 1936, when I was five years old, she sent me to my room at or close to 7 P.M. for using four-letter words while trimming the Christmas tree. I do not recall that.

The assertion is absolutely false that when I came home from high school with an A-minus she demanded an explanation for the minus.

It has been alleged that she spoiled me with protectionism, because I was the youngest child and therefore the most vulnerable to attack from overhead—an assertion that I cannot confirm or confute, except to say that facts don't lie.

We lived only a few blocks from the elementary school and I

routinely ate lunch at home. It is reported that the following dialogue and ensuing action occurred on January 22, 1941:

"Eat your sandwich."

"I don't want to eat my sandwich."

"I made that sandwich, and you are going to eat it, Mister Man. You filled yourself up on penny candy on the way home, and now you're not hungry."

"I'm late. I have to go. I'll eat the sandwich on the way back to school."

"Promise?"

"Promise."

Allegedly, I went up the street with the sandwich in my hand and buried it in a snowbank in front of Dr. Wright's house. My mother, holding back the curtain in the window of the side door, was watching. She came out in the bitter cold, wearing only a light dress, ran to the snowbank, dug out the sandwich, chased me up Nassau Street, and rammed the sandwich down my throat, snow and all. I do not recall any detail of that story. I believe it to be a total fabrication.

There was the case of the missing Cracker Jack at Lindel's corner store. Flimsy evidence pointed to Mrs. McPhee's smallest child. It has been averred that she laid the guilt on with the following words: "'Like mother like son' is a saying so true, the world will judge largely of mother by you." It has been asserted that she immediately repeated that proverb three times, and also recited it on other occasions too numerous to count. I have absolutely no recollection of her saying that about the Cracker Jack or any other controlled substance.

We have now covered everything even faintly unsavory that has been reported about this person in ninety-nine years, and even those items are a collection of rumors, half-truths, prevarications, false allegations, inaccuracies, innuendos, and canards.

This is the mother who—when Alfred Knopf wrote her twenty-two-year-old son a letter saying, "The readers' reports in the case of your manuscript would not be very helpful, and I think might discourage you completely"—said, "Don't listen to Alfred Knopf. Who does Alfred Knopf think he is, anyway? Someone should go in there and k-nock his block off." To the best of my recollection, that is what she said.

I also recall her taking me, on or about March 8, my birthday, to the theatre in New York every year, beginning in childhood. I remember those journeys as if they were today. I remember "A Connecticut Yankee." Wednesday, March 8, 1944. Evidently, my father had written for the tickets, because she and I sat in the last row of the second balcony. Mother knew what to do about that. She gave me for my birthday an elegant spyglass, sufficient in power to bring the Connecticut Yankee back from Vermont. I sat there watching the play through my telescope, drawing as many guffaws from the surrounding audience as the comedy on the stage.

On one of those theatre days—when I was eleven or twelve— I asked her if we could start for the city early and go out to LaGuardia Field to see the comings and goings of airplanes. The temperature was well below the freeze point and the March winds were so blustery that the wind-chill factor was forty below zero. Or seemed to be. My mother figured out how to take the subway to a stop in Jackson Heights and a bus from there—a feat I am unable to duplicate to this day. At LaGuardia, she accompanied me to the observation deck and stood there in the icy wind for at least an hour, maybe two, while I, spellbound, watched the

DC-3s coming in on final, their wings flapping in the gusts. When we at last left the observation deck, we went downstairs into the terminal, where she bought me what appeared to be a black rubber ball but on closer inspection was a pair of hollow hemispheres hinged on one side and folded together. They contained a silk parachute. Opposite the hinge, each hemisphere had a small nib. A piece of string wrapped round and round the two nibs kept the ball closed. If you threw it high into the air, the string unwound and the parachute blossomed. If you sent it up with a tennis racquet, you could put it into the clouds. Not until the development of the multi-megabyte hard disk would the world ever know such a fabulous toy. Folded just so, the parachute never failed. Always, it floated back to you—silkily, beautifully—to start over and float back again. Even if you abused it, whacked it really hard—gracefully, lightly, it floated back to you.

SEASON ON THE CHALK

The massive chalk of Europe lies below the English Channel, under much of northern France, under bits of Germany and Scandinavia, under the Limburg Province of the Netherlands, and—from Erith Reach to Gravesend—under fifteen miles of the lower Thames. My grandson Tommaso appears out of somewhere and picks up a cobble from the bottom of the Thames. The tide is out. The flats are broad between the bank and the water. Small boats, canted, are at rest on the riverbed. Others, farther out on the wide river, are moored afloat—skiffs, sloops, a yawl or two. Tommaso is ten. The rock in his hand is large but light. He breaks it against the revetment bordering the Gordon Promenade, in the Riverside Leisure Area, with benches and lawns under oaks and chestnuts, prams and children, picnics under way, newspapers spread like sails, and, far up the bank, a stall selling ice cream. He cracks the cobble into jagged pieces, which are whiter than snow. Chalked graffiti line the revetment and have attracted the attention of Tommaso, who now starts his own with the letter "R."

One of the stranded skiffs is painted a bright orange, and large letters on its tilted-up side say "The Crown and Thistle Public House." A yellow skiff, also askew, says "The Terrace Tavern Public House." A red one represents "The George Inn, Queen Street." When the tide has turned and the skiffs are up on the water, the pubs race one another. This is the beginning of the Thames Estuary, where, in centuries gone, a thousand ships would be anchored, waiting to go up into London.

"O"

Tommaso is taking his time with these letters, because he is using an ambitious font. The lines that have formed the "R" and the "O" are four inches wide. An armada of swans, in single file, swims out from near shore and toward the center of the river—thirty-eight swans. Here, above the chalk, is where the Nellie, a cruising yawl, swung to her anchor, waiting for the tide to turn, while

> the tanned sails of the barges drifting up with the tide seemed to stand still in red clusters of canvas sharply peaked, with gleams of varnished sprits. A haze rested on the low shores that ran out to sea in vanishing flatness. The air was dark above Gravesend, and farther back still seemed condensed into a mournful gloom, brooding motionless over the biggest, and the greatest, town on earth.

Marlow then described to his friends on the yawl's deck his journey to the heart of darkness.

"C"

Tommaso goes to Fulham Prep, and recently bet a number of his classmates a pound apiece that he would not win the Form Prize. He won the Form Prize and went bankrupt.

"K"

With his rendering of ROCK, he has won the admiration of his grandfather for his evident devotion to earth science. He has also drawn a crowd. Average age: seven. Quietly and respectfully, they watch this older artist, his concentration undisturbed. He leaves some space and begins a new word, with another "O." In the Nellie's time, the last decade of the nineteenth century, the river here at Gravesend was full of troop ships, cargo ships, and emigrant ships, waiting on tides. And more than tides. They sometimes waited for weeks before sailing. On hulks and barges, boatmen serving the ships lived on the river with their families and with their cats, dogs, chickens, sheep, and cows. Now downriver comes the Tor Belgia, out of London, with a six-deck rear house, followed by the Arco Humber, spewing bilge, a floating cadaver of ulcerated rust. Pilot boats, ratlike, scurry away from these tankers. Docked across the river in Tilbury is the Russian ship Annoya, of nine Cyrillic letters and a six-deck house. A motor yacht goes by, so elegant that it appears to be lost—seems to be seeking Lake Geneva.

"N"

ROCK ON. I didn't say he was William Butler Yeats. He is Tommaso U. P. McPhee, son of Luca Passaleva and Jenny McPhee, brother of six-year-old Leandro McPhee, who is the least quiet member of Tommaso's attentive crowd. With a large white "S," a second line begins, and gradually becomes SKI-MAN, a character in a screenplay that Tommaso has written and intends to direct. Backdropping this scene, up the bank above the prams and the Sunday papers, are the parapets and big guns of an eighteenth-century fort, vastly amplified in the nineteenth by Chinese Gordon of Khartoum, and meant to blow out of service anything afloat that might threaten London. Tommaso adds a peace symbol to his completed graffito.

East of Gravesend is a town called Chalk, with a thoroughfare called Chalk Road, a barber's called Chalk Cuts, and a neighborhood called Chalk Park, where mobile homes have tile roofs. In a cottage still standing on Chalk Road, Charles Dickens spent the honeymoon of his ill-fated marriage, picking at "The Pickwick Papers." The M2 runs on the chalk as far as Faversham, where the chalk drifts southeast to Deal and Dover and the Kentish cliffs above the English Channel. From the water, in the approach to Dover, the chalk cliffs under their cap of vegetation are like the filling in a broken wafer, a cross-sectional exposure of the nation's basement. More resistant than some rocks to the effects of weather, the chalk stands high, and its landform suggests on a magnified scale the swells and waves in the water beside it. This karst topography, as it is called, carries on toward London as the North Downs, and from any number of its high points the view to the south goes uninterrupted for thirty-odd miles before it is stopped by an east-west band of high chalk that more than suggests a range of mountains. The reciprocal scene, northward, from Devil's Dyke or Ditchling Beacon or almost anywhere on the ridgeline of the South Downs, was described by John Constable in 1824 as "perhaps the most grand and affecting natural landscape in the world—and consequently a scene the most unfit for a picture." Easily, instantly, your eyes take in a thousand square miles of low terrain in pastel greens and browns, a region too broad to be called a valley but known since Anglo-Saxon England as the Weald. "It is the business of a painter not to contend with nature," the surprising Constable explained, "but to make something out of nothing, in attempting which he must almost of necessity become poetical." And, true to his artistic standards, this surpassing English landscape painter sketched almost nothing of the hackneyed panorama of the Weald.

The South Downs Way, a public and ancient footpath through

fields and over stiles and under notably few trees, stays up on the highest ground between Eastbourne and Winchester—a hundred miles. In billows of chalk, the Downs rise from the sea and go on rising northward to elevations approaching a thousand feet, culminating in the escarpment that plunges to the Weald. The declivity is so steep that funiculars have been built to ascend it. Spring-line villages developed at the base, where waters come out of the chalk. To the Anglo-Saxons a weald was a woodland and a mountain was a dun. Words that were good enough for Caedmon and Bede are not for recycling now. So the Downs are up and the Weald is down, beyond the spring-line towns.

East of Ditchling Beacon, where bonfires signalled the approach of the Armada, the South Downs Way passes close to Breaky Bottom. This is a small, deep, roughly circular valley countersunk in the highest chalk, walled in on all sides by rims about a mile across—an enclosed coombe. A form of dry chalk valley, it has no stream. Not many miles from Brighton and Hove, it seems nonetheless as remote as a valley in Nevada. Sequestered, secretive, sheltered from its windswept environs, it has an intimate and fairly level floor that is covered with orderly rows of vines. I would like to say that I arrived on foot, coming off the ridge, but I was actually a passenger in an aqua Audi driven by H. G. T. P. Doyne-Ditmas, of Brighton. We came up past Piddinghoe on the River Ouse and on by steep fields full of rolled hay to a whitish chalk track, pitted and rutted, extending a mile and a half beyond a sign that said "No Through Road."

We descend, helically, and park under a horse chestnut near a flint wall, a house, a flint barn. We step into a scene of utter quiet.

Call this the most peaceful place in Europe—willows over the flint garden wall, a line of poplars against the sky, cattle like brown pebbles far up the circumvallate grazings, fewer than few human inhabitants, proprietor nowhere in sight. He is in his kitchen, conferring with a buyer.

While we wait, we walk among the grapes—Chardonnay, Pinot Noir, and Seyval Blanc, as Doyne-Ditmas is aware, because he discovered Breaky Bottom some years ago, and tasted the still and the sparkling wines, and later rang up a former colleague of his who had become Deputy Private Secretary to the Queen, and suggested that Her Majesty's government buy and serve this patriotic wine, especially the generic champagne. Think of it— English champagne! From the Palace, the former colleague said thank you very much but the government already are a Breaky Bottom customer, and the champagne—or, strictly speaking, the *méthode champenoise* sparkling wine—is much in use "for government entertainment, including entertainment by the Queen."

Doyne-Ditmas has a fraternal niece named Caroline, who was Princess Anne's head groom during Princess Anne's competitive equestrian years and is now one of Anne's ladies-in-waiting. At the equestrian events, Caroline was sometimes asked by Special Branch police officers if she was "related to Mr. Doyne-Ditmas of the Box." She affirmed that she was. The Box is MI5.

Peter Hall, proprietor and *viticulteur*, comes out of the house, says goodbye to his customer under the chestnut, and turns to us. He is wearing a white T-shirt, and he's a man of middle height, with friendly eyes, an intelligent pate, a fringe of white hair, a tanned face, a white beard, and a talent for non-stop talking. First off, he orients us to our surroundings by quoting "A Midsummer

Night's Dream." Demetrius to Helena: "I'll run from thee and hide me in the brakes."

Next he tells us that his mother was French, his father English, and his brother died of AIDS in New York. His father was the author of a memoir on fly-fishing in Scotland. His brother is commemorated on the labels of Breaky Bottom's Cuvée Rémy Alexandre. Peter Hall says "vinn yard," accent on the "yard." "I've always liked small scale," he continues. "I'm happy to be the owner-driver of what I do." At the moment, he has only about fifty thousand bottles laid up in various stages of development. Recent government orders have brought him "thirteen thousand nine hundred pounds of taxpayers' money." We go into his flint barn. His fermentation tanks are from Italy. His wine press, French, looks expensive and a great deal less nauseating than a stomp of bare feet. It is a stainless cylinder with an interior bag. Come harvest, grapes go into the cylinder. The bag swells with compressed air and squeezes the grapes. The air goes out; then the bag refills, and squeezes the grapes a little more. How much did the thing cost?

"Twenty-five thousand quid," Peter Hall says.

Nobody says "quid" anymore, Doyne-Ditmas is silently reflecting.

The Breaky Bottom cave is not down in the chalk, as one would expect. It is a large space in the barn—sealed, insulated, firmly kept at twelve degrees Celsius by a pricey air-conditioner. How pricey?

"Ten thousand quid. To burrow into the chalk would have been a hundred thousand quid."

Peter Hall came here in the nineteen-sixties on an internship after taking an agricultural degree at Newcastle University. Breaky Bottom was a wheat and cattle farm. He lived "in a tiny cottage and worked for the farmer." After his year was up, he asked if he could stay another year. "As long as you don't talk so much," the farmer said. Peter married the farmer's daughter. They produced four children, and the farmer offered him a tenancy. Now the marriage is in the past, Peter has a different companion, and the farmer is dead.

On the six planted acres at the bottom of the dry chalk valley, the behavior of water is unpredictable. The coombe is, in effect, a giant cistern collecting rain, of which there is no shortage. But chalk is porous, and, in Peter's words, "the chalk takes all the water." When it receives so much that it can hold no more, this streamless basin develops a full-bore flood. Such an event occurs roughly once in five years, leaving almost enough time for a vintner to become complacent.

"I've flooded five times," Peter says.

What does that do to the vines?

"It buggers them up. Vines like their feet dry." Just as vines do around Reims and Épernay, in the province of Champagne, in northeastern France, where the wines owe their speciality in large part to the chalk that holds the roots of the vines. Chalk, like limestone, endows a fertile soil. The province has two principal areas, with differing bedrock—Wet Champagne, on sands and clays, and Dry Champagne, on younger chalk—and the Taittingers, Mumms, and Piper-Heidsiecks come off the chalk of Dry Champagne. Relatively dry Champagne. The chalk feeds water to the vines.

The kitchen in Breaky Bottom's farmhouse trails modern kitchens by about a hundred years and is a hundred times as pleasant, with its apparatus in heavy black iron, its slanting window light, its glasses and bottles on the blue oilcloth of a large wooden table. Listening to Peter Hall, we sit and sip, appreciate, spit. A pitcher is in service as a glass spittoon. A 2003 still wine is "like sucking a lemon at half time," we are told. "It's refreshing, zestful." A 1996 Müller-Thurgau is "elegantly shaped, like a Gewürztraminer, but it has backed off from there." The main events are the champagnes (a term he doesn't use). "This young '03 is pretty zesty, sharp, punchy stuff." This 1999 is "more rounded, bigger flavor—quite a drink. . . . I'm growing Chardonnay, Pinot Noir, and Seyval Blanc now principally with fizz in mind, to see what comes off this chalk." Already, his production is "preponderantly fizzy," and soon, he says, he might decide "to go a hundred per cent fizz."

"Why would you do that? The still wines are very good."

"If I had a herd of goats, I could sell milk to the local health-food store. If I made cheese, I could sell it for three times as much."

During the tasting, Peter has been smoking a rolled smoke. He rolls another. After taking the wines in his mouth, he gives them a good hard squish, making a gravelly, smoky sound like a bullfrog.

For my part, I am not ejecting a whole lot of what I am sipping, and I am getting a little drunk. Doyne-Ditmas, through all, has been patient, observant, unreadable. We came here before lunchtime intending to spend an hour, and it is now nearing three in the afternoon. Doyne-Ditmas and I have known each other since we went to Deerfield Academy, in western Massachusetts. He was sent there by the English-Speaking Union and stood out from everyone else as "the English exchange student."

He had no cover then. He was the least anonymous student in the school. We concocted a plan that four years later I would enroll in his college at the University of Cambridge, which I did.

"I am now principally a sparkling-wine maker," Peter Hall says once more, after spitting out some '99. More broadly, he asserts that it is only a matter of time before "the U.K. will become prominent in sparkling wine." After all, Épernay is virtually next door, just a bit down the chalk. "From here, Champagne is two hundred and fifty miles southeast and you can virtually spit there."

From Breaky Bottom out through Beachy Head, under the Channel, and up into Picardy, and on past Arras and Amiens, the chalk is continuous to Reims and Épernay. To drive the small roads and narrow lanes of Champagne is to drive the karstic downlands of Sussex and Surrey, the smoothly bold topography of Kentish chalk—the French ridges, long and soft, the mosaic fields and woodlots, the chalk boulders by the road in villages like Villeneuve-l'Archêveque. Here the French fieldstone is chalk, and the quarry stone—white drywalls, white barns, white churches. The chalk church of Orvilliers-Saint-Julien. The chalk around the sunflowers of Rigny-la-Nonneuse. The chalkstone walls at Marcilly-le-Hayer. Near Épernay, even the cattle are white. Vines like green corduroy run for miles up the hillsides in rows perpendicular to the contours, and the tops of the vines are so accordant that the vines up close look more like green fences, and the storky, long-legged tractors of Champagne straddle rows and run above the grapes.

This is a region of well over three hundred villages, spread mainly around the flaring skirts of the Montagne de Reims and below its dense upland forests. Verzy, Verzenay, Mailly-Champagne, Mutigny, Ay, Hautvillers, Châtillon-sur-Marne—each village is, among other things, a cru. Forty-four villages are premiers crus. Seventeen are grands crus. A couple of highways run past the villages, and small paved roads among them, but the lanes that traverse and connect the vineyards are for the most part little more than two ruts of scraped-off chalk. Small roadcuts in the steeper slopes among the vines expose above the chalk the sands, clays, and marls of younger age that have washed down off the mountain and veneered the chalk, resulting in what is looked upon as elixir soil for the signature wine of this province. Up in the vineyards over Ay, a Sunday afternoon in steady rain, the green vines glisten, while water on the chalk roads runs like milk. Your car goes up to its hubcaps in milk.

In the Église Abbatiale, in Hautvillers, only a few kilometres and a few hundred thousand vines above Ay, lie the bones of St. Nivard, some fourteen hundred years since they began forming inside his young body. He founded this Benedictine abbey, which, through centuries, has rung with quiet, as its church does today, if you are not disquieted by the low recorded sound of the Twenty-first Piano Concerto. This may be one of the few places on earth that could do without Mozart, introducing, as he does, a sense of sideshow in the vaulted space. Nivard's bones are viewable, casketed in glass, while on black stone set in the floor nearby are the words "Hic Jacet Dom Petrus Perignon . . . Plenus Paternoque Imprimis in Pauperes Amore." In the seventeenth century, Pierre Pérignon became the cellarer of the abbey, not exactly the sommelier, but not inexactly, either. His job was to gather provisions of all kinds, including wine, for the brothers' table. He was a skilled blender, according to the geologist James E. Wilson's "Terroir: The Role of Geology, Climate, and Culture in the Making of French Wines," but, contrary to Pérignon's worldwide reputation, he did not add to the wines the magic bits of sugar and yeast that enhance carbonation in the second fermentation and result in champagne as we know it and he did not. Later, he acquired the title Dom, or Master, and what is thought to have been his way is what is meant by the words *méthode champenoise* and *méthode traditionelle* on the labels of American, Argentine, Australian, South African, Greek, Chilean, Israeli, Latvian, Spanish, English, and Canadian champagnes.

While the landscapes of Dry Champagne bear more than a cousinly resemblance to the Downs of southern England, the underground scene in Reims, Ay, and Épernay does not call to mind an air-conditioned barn. Deep in the French chalk are hundreds of kilometres of tunnels—straight-line tunnels, curvilinear tunnels, tunnels on various levels crisscrossing other tunnels—holding more than a billion bottles of champagne. In Épernay, on the much embattled Marne, the mansions and offices of Pol Roger, Perrier Jouet, Mercier, Moët & Chandon, and others are lined up on the two sides of the Avenue de Champagne and over something like a Russian coal mine. On three levels, Moët & Chandon alone has eighteen miles of tunnels. The white walls are cool, sticky, and damp, belying the dryness overhead. The name Champagne stems from Campania, of whose dusty fields Romans were reminded when they came here. The porous chalk absorbs rain as fast as it falls, and the year-round temperature down in the caves is wintry.

Dimly lighted passages reach so far into a mournful and brooding gloom that the eye is stopped not by rock but by darkness. Along the sides, as in a catacomb, are vaults, crypts—a seemingly endless series of crypts, typically six feet by sixteen feet, like one-fifth of your one-room apartment. The tight space notwithstanding, in each crypt lie some twenty thousand bottles of champagne. There are workrooms down here in the chalk, and among the many talents of the workers the most technologically advanced is riddling. It is two centuries old. When yeasted and sugared wines have lain flat long enough to build up their sparkle, the yeast and other sediments inside the bottles must be removed; and how does one do that without losing the bubbles? Enter the *veuve* Clicquot, the enological Edison, widowed in 1805 and left in control of her husband's Remois winery, where she became, in effect, the first riddler. She placed the ready bottles on an A-framed rack, tilting them neck down, and she gradually steepened the incline as weeks went by. Once a day or so—to dislodge the yeast from the bottle walls and to stir up the sediments—she gave each bottle a sharp turn to the right and a sharp turn back to the left, then stopped its rotation a little farther along than it had been. In the annals of addiction, not even whole Greek islands terraced to the sky in vines, or Falernian vats holding enough wine to intoxicate the Tenth Legion—not even the great Heidelberg tun—could be more emblematic than a portrait of a riddler in the chalk. One riddler can turn thirty thousand bottles a day, and with each turn, and each additional degree of tilt, the grubby items in near-suspension in the otherwise diaphanous fluid gravitate into the neck of the bottle. After eight weeks or so, a palpable plug is filling the neck—a plug as soft and repulsive as phlegm. The neck is locally frozen, as if by a dermatologist. The bottle is turned upright and opened. The carbon dioxide in the champagne drives out the frozen plug, and the bottle is swiftly capped with a wired-down cork mushroom. Machines controlled by computers do most of the riddling now, but when the machines break down, as they do, riddlers are here to take over.

Moët & Chandon has about twenty-five hundred acres of its own grapes and buys a great many more from villages around the region. The company uses two skinless reds and a white, and generally begins its champagnes with still wines of three successive years. The top of the line is labelled Dom Pérignon. It is made only from Chardonnay and Pinot Noir, is nearly a hundred per cent from grands crus, and is aged seven years. This is not the Médoc. In your flute, what will matter is not a unique vineyard but the status of the various places where the grapes grew on the chalk.

In 1822, the Belgian stratigrapher J. J. d'Omalius d'Halloy, working for the French government, put a name on the chalk of Europe which would come to represent an ungainly share of geologic time. Collectively, d'Halloy called the English downlands and the white sea cliffs and the bottom of the Channel and Dry Champagne—and so forth—Le Terrain Crétacé. Chalky it surely was, and soon the word not only made the jump from adjective to adjectival noun but also from geologic system to geologic period—from rock to time. With the arguable exception of the Carboniferous, the Cretaceous is the only period in the forty-six hundred million years of the earth's history that was directly named for a rock.

While nineteenth-century geologists were able to establish the relative ages of various formations by noting what lay over and under what, they had no way of measuring the amount of time the units represented. Radiometrics now suggest that the Jurassic Period, which precedes the Cretaceous and was named for a mountain range, ended about a hundred and forty-five million years ago. Then on came the Cretaceous, with its flying reptiles, its rudistid clams, its titanosaurs, dromaeosaurs, elasmosaurs, duck-billed and ostrich dinosaurs, and introductory flowering plants, not to mention Triceratops, Tyrannosaurus rex, and all the marine invertebrates that disappeared in the Cretaceous Extinction, sixty-five million years ago, a date better known to modern schoolchildren than 1492. In the Cretaceous was more time than there has been since the Cretaceous. The Paleocene, Eocene, Oligocene, Miocene, Pliocene, Pleistocene, and Holocene add up only to four-fifths of the eighty million years of the Cretaceous. The chalk it is named for developed during roughly half of Cretaceous time—temporally the more recent half, stratigraphically the upper half. The chalk is made of the calcareous remains of microscopic marine plants and animals that lived in the water column and sank after death—slower than riddled yeast—in epicontinental seas. The chalk accumulated at the rate of about one millimetre in a century, and the thickness got past three hundred metres in some thirty-five million years.

The beds that rise closest to the date of the extinction are known in French geology as Le Crétacé Supérieur, in England as the Upper Chalk. This is the chalk of the vineyards and Downs, the chalk of the Champagne cellars, and it wraps around the Paris Basin and down to the Touraine. But then it disappears as the country continues in older lithologies, in collisional juxtapositions of magmas and metamorphics, of Precambrian, Cambrian, Ordovician, and Devonian rocks. Oddly, though, in isolation, Le Crétacé Supérieur outcrops in Cognac. Five hundred beeline kilometres from Reims, the chalk of a couple of the uppermost Cretaceous stages is concentrated under vineyards east and southeast of town. The spirit that derives from these vineyards is labelled "Grande Champagne cognac." Next door, where the soil is a bit less favorable, the product is labelled "Petite Champagne cognac." There are many other cognacs, but none is superior, Cretaceously or otherwise, to the champagne cognacs.

In the nineteenth century, the long unwieldy geologic periods were subdivided into stages and ages—respectively of rock and time. Three of the four highest levels of the Cretaceous are the (successively younger) Coniacian, Santonian, and Campanian. These are universal in the scientific vocabulary, applying to whatever happens to be of identical age anywhere on the planet. Coniacian is a reference to Cognac. Santonian refers to the town of Saintes, fifteen miles up the road. Campanian, of course, is a nod to Champagne. Imagine these names being tossed about at the Chinese Geological Survey. Cognac is on the Charente, which flows along a fault line that trends east-west. On the south side of the river are the Grande Champagne vineyards of the late Cretaceous. The north side is Jurassic and not in the conversation.

The youngest of all levels of Cretaceous chalk was identified by the stratigrapher André Dumont in 1849 and called Maastrichtian. The adjective refers to the Dutch town where, as it happens, the euro would come to be (in 1991) and the European Union would form. It is the provincial capital of Limburg, which hangs down eccentrically from the southeastern corner of the rest of the Netherlands. The river Meuse, which rises in France and flows six hundred miles to the North Sea, becomes the river Maas when it crosses into Holland. Maastricht was where the

Romans forded the Maas. Much of its bedrock is Maastrichtian chalk.

On the Onze Lieve Vrouweplein, a square in the old core of Maastricht, is the frankly modern Hotel Derlon, which is evidently as unembarrassed to be looking out on ancient and medieval Europe through large rectangles of plate glass as it is justly proud of the Roman ruins in its basement. They were discovered in 1983 during the hotel's reconstruction, and they include massive foundation walls of quarried chalk and a water well surrounded by chalk blocks as much as two feet thick. Carefully excavated archeologically, these Roman artifacts are as well protected as they would be had they been carted off by the British Museum. Do not enter. Do not touch. Just sit down at a ruinside table and dine in this hallowed space, which the hotel calls Museumkelder Derlon. Maastricht has other Roman vestiges, and they also are made of quarried chalk. For many centuries, Maastricht was a walled city, and large segments of its sixteen-foot chalk walls still stand. Maastricht remains intimate, self-contained, vintage European—a city of chalk basilicas and chalk churches, one of which is eleven centuries old. Where was all that chalk quarried? Surely not under the city. Have you been to the *grotten* in Sint Pietersberg, just five miles up the river? No? Party of five? Take one of the *bootsfahrten*.

The boat is long and mahoganied with waiters and a bar, and casts off from the left bank above the Sint Servaasbrug, the oldest bridge in the Netherlands. At this same site was a Roman bridge, which lasted about a thousand years and fell into the river in the twelve-seventies. Sint Servaasbrug, with seven piers, dates from 1280. The boat swings under it, and up the center of a long reach through the city, the right bank glassy and corporate, the left bank's skyline tiled, turreted, and ecclesiastical. The left bank is to our right; the right bank is to our left. Such river runes are not beyond the grasp of Livia Svenvold McPhee, who is six and quick to learn, but they're off the scale for her two-year-old brother, Jasper, and, dare I say it, their father and mother, Mark Svenvold and Martha McPhee. The breeze is cool on the open deck, and the boat is soon running past saturated fields that resemble the fens of Cambridgeshire which are also on the chalk. Jet Skis circle the boat, and weave Olympic rings around slow-moving barges full of crushed cars. Other barges, carrying ores and grains, are everywhere on the river, as are private cabin boats, nosing around the barges like pretentious tugs.

A steep but modest hill comes into view off the left bank: literally, on Dutch maps, a mountain—Sint Pietersberg. What the berg is made of is not a great mystery in this province. E.N.C.I.—Eerste Nederlandse Cement Industrie—is carved into its base, where the Comité d'Étude du Maastrichtian confirmed this place as the type locality of the final stage of the Cretaceous. We have come to see an operation that is a good deal older than E.N.C.I., though, and we climb the hill past and above E.N.C.I. until we see what could easily be mistaken for the entrance to Carlsbad Caverns, or to Luray Caverns, or to Mammoth Cave. With the difference that this excavation is absolutely unnatural. The word *grotten* is used for its subterranean galleries—the Grotten Sint Pietersberg—but this is not a cave, or a series of caves. It's a mine. Specifically, it's a chalk quarry—an intermittent source of building stone across a scale of time approaching twenty-one hundred years. The *grotten* actually are much like the tunnels of

Moët & Chandon, which—heaven help us—are called caves but also are not caves.

For well casings, foundations, fortifications, and bathhouses, among other things, the Romans were the first to go into the mountain, and they did so for several hundred years, giving up the quarry in the fourth century. Its rock is a less than pure-white chalk, tanned by enough clay to be called a marl. In a group, you follow a guide with two electric lanterns, suspended from bails like railroad lanterns. He hands one to the last guidee in line, then leads the way into darkness, cracking jokes in English. His name is Leon Frissen. He is short, stocky, balding, and friendly. You follow him down and down through a gallery system, and if you've ever been in a salt mine the place reminds you of a salt mine. The constant temperature is ten degrees Celsius and you shiver. Now you are about thirty-five metres below the surface. The gallery walls are seven metres high. The lantern light is the only light. It throws awkward, lurching shadows. Seeing me struggle to write notes, Frissen takes a flashlight out of his pocket and gives it to me. Rounding a corner, we look down a straight corridor into a mournful and infinite gloom. Frissen says the corridor goes on for several kilometres before the next bend. He says there are three hundred and fifty kilometres of galleries in and beyond the mountain, hewn, by *blokbrekers*, with three tools: chisel, hammer, and saw. The quarrying resumed in the thirteenth century and continued until 1926.

Allied pilots, shot down during the Second World War, were taken into the tunnels and led underground to Resistance forces in nearby Belgium. The route was known as the Pilots Line. On tunnel walls, it was blazed by drawings of doves. In the Sint

Pietersberg galleries, you see doves not only on the walls but also on the thick and natural pillars of chalk left standing to prevent the collapse of the mine. From 1942 to 1945, Dutch museums hid more than seven hundred works of art inside the mountain, including Vermeer's "The Little Street" and Rembrandt's "The Night Watch," a huge canvas (fifteen square metres) that spent the rest of the war rolled up as a stalagmite. After surface telephone lines were destroyed by German bombs, a line was run through the *grotten* keeping connections open with Belgium and northern France. Maastrichtians and other people of the province hid in the mountain, especially while battle raged through Limburg. You see a niche chapel far underground, and Stations of the Cross. There was a bakery, a hospital, and three churches, two of them Roman Catholic. Twelve thousand people were inside the mountain in late summer, 1944. Maastricht was freed by Allied troops, mostly American, on the fourteenth of September. A few kilometres east of the mountain, in the Netherlands American Cemetery, eighty-three hundred soldiers are buried in the chalk.

Graffiti in the tunnels in the mountain—drawings, advertisements, people's names—can be arranged as a sort of timescale of the ages of quarrying, just as the scale of the ages of the Cretaceous rise through Berriasian, Valanginian, Hauterivian, Barremian, Aptian, Albian, Cenomanian, Turonian, Coniacian, Santonian, Campanian, and Maastrichtian time.

There are names on the walls from 1551.

Among swinging shadows in lantern light, the name of Don Ferdinand Álvarez de Toledo, Duke of Alba, appears with the date 1570. (His headquarters were on the mountain. Spanish troops massacred thousands of Maastrichtians on a single day in 1579.)

Someone called Olivier left his name in the *grotten* in 1660.

As did Ianno in 1681, with a word about the quality of his oil.
(Ianno was a merchant. To the *blokbrekers*, he sold linseed oil for
their lamps.)

Rosa de Horlon was here, her name on the wall: 14 *mei* 1781.

Napoleon Bonaparte 1803.

Martha: "Why was Napoleon here?"

Guide: "Why are you here?"

Martha considers this an inadequate answer.

Too busy scribbling, I keep my question to myself: If Napoleon knew what was inside the mountain, and other tourists
toured the quarry in the nineteenth century, why were the Nazis
unaware of the Maastrichtian refuge and the Pilots Line? (According to Rik Valkenburg's "Ondergronds Verzet: Illegale Trans-
porten door de Grotten van de Sint Pietersberg-Maastricht in
1940–1944," Maastrichtians convinced the Germans that it had
become physically impossible to move people or goods to Belgium through the mountain. They took the head of the local
Gestapo on a selective tour of the *grotten* and drove home the
point. German soldiers did occasionally patrol parts of the vast
subterranean maze, but the Resistance knew their routes and
schedules. Travellers on the Pilots Line shrank back into lightless
caverns.)

There are names on the walls from 1854.

From the eighteen-seventies, there's an ad for Bols gin.

A remarkably detailed, beautifully drawn, anonymous charcoal
landscape is dated 1904.

Ferocious mosasaur, sketched on a tunnel wall in 1907—the
big-headed, long-toothed, long-bodied predatory reptile that lived
in the Cretaceous ocean and its epicontinental seas. "Mosasaur,"
misleadingly, means reptile of the river Maas—actually a marine

creature, not riverine, discovered inside Sint Pietersberg in the eighteenth century, fifty years before the earliest description of dinosaurs. Mosasaurs were as much as fifty feet long, swimming like snakes toward the Cretaceous Extinction.

On the chalk near the mosasaur: a 1948 drawing of the Dutch royal family, the present queen, Beatrix, as a princess ten years old.

Returning to sunlight, we start to descend the hill, and Livia has a question for her mother.

Livia: "Why was granddaddy writing all those notes?"

Martha: "Ask him."

Livia: "Granddaddy, why were you writing all those notes?"

Scandinavian blond, beautiful beyond reason, as swift of mind as she is beautiful, etcetera, etcetera, Livia is nonetheless not yet in first grade. She will not know from Maastrichtian time. In explanatory dialogue with her, who could use a term like Cretaceous Extinction, let alone trace the Upper Chalk to the end of Cretaceous time?

Granddaddy: "Well, Livia, let's see. You've heard of dinosaurs, right?"

Livia (evenly): "Yes."

Granddaddy: "They got bigger and bigger, and there came a time when they all disappeared from the earth. Right?"

Livia: "Yes."

Granddaddy: "Have you ever wondered what killed them?"

Livia: "Asteroid, or volcano."

As we go down the mountain, I keep looking at her in wonder, yes, but in fading disbelief. Her reply to my question actually adds up to something more than a good story to tell about a beloved six-year-old granddaughter. It is also an index to conventional wisdom, and to the speed of its development. The hypothesis that a big asteroid—a so-called bolide, or Apollo object—hit the earth sixty-five million years ago and sent up enough particulate matter to darken the atmosphere and cut off the food chain was published in 1980. It was surprising news. The physicist Freeman Dyson referred to it at the time as "the most interesting piece of science" he had read in ten years. Now a freshly turned-out kindergarten graduate lists it first among the causes of the death of the dinosaurs. And so, I think, would a majority of people on the planet who are aware, to whatever extent, of the Cretaceous Extinction. What was unknown not many years ago is conventional wisdom now. The 1980 paper, in *Science*, reported the research and conclusions of Walter Alvarez, a geologist, and his father, Luis, who won the Nobel Prize in Physics in 1968. Their idea stemmed from the globally widespread presence at the Cretaceous-Tertiary stratigraphic boundary of certain platinum-group metals rare on the earth but common in meteorites and other extraterrestrial objects. The crater of a very large asteroid was later identified in and around northern Yucatán, its impact of appropriate age. Walter Alvarez told the story in a lively and well-received book called "T. rex and the Crater of Doom." By now, the discovery has become so well established that it has made its way down through the grades and even into preschool.

Not everyone has become a subscriber, though—not even the population of every West Side kindergarten, as one could see in Livia's response, "Asteroid, or volcano." I wish she had said "volcanism," but what can I do? She isn't seven yet. Before 1980, a number of other researchers matched the Cretaceous Extinction to the vast outpouring of flood basalts that solidified as the Deccan Traps. From countless fissures, at least forty-five hundred trillion tons of incandescent lava poured out across more than two hundred thousand square miles of what is now western India. Those eruptions—so the "volcano" hypothesis goes—altered the entire atmosphere and broke the food chain, with the result that some two-thirds of all species on earth perished, a fact that is legible in the fossil record. Flood basalts of such magnitude occur when geophysical hot spots first manifest themselves on the earth's surface. The heat is escaping from regions in or near the earth's core, and it rises through the mantle in a thermal plume that melts a vast quantity of mantle and crust and drives it out at the top. A hot spot lasts about a hundred million years. While a tectonic plate—a thin shell in this context—slides over the hot spot, it is repeatedly penetrated by the plume, like a piece of cloth by the needle of a sewing machine. Over time, many hot spots have come and gone, leaving vestiges like Bermuda and the Bahama Platform. The Musician Seamounts, in the North Pacific Ocean, are the track of a dead hot spot. About twenty major ones are active in the modern world, such as Hawaii, Iceland, Mt. Cameroon, Tahiti, Madeira, and Yellowstone, which began in Oregon and Washington as the Columbia River flood basalts and has stitched an east-moving track while the North American Plate, moving west, has slid over its penetrating plume. "Traps" is a term that derives from a Swedish word that means stair steps. It describes the appearance—on the Malabar coast, in the Columbia Gorge, etc.—of successive lava flows that harden as basalt.

The Cretaceous Extinction ranks second to the Permian Extinction—at the end of the Paleozoic Era, about two hundred and fifty-one million years before the present—in which ninety-nine per cent of all animals on the earth, of every size, from large to microscopic, were killed. At the Paleozoic-Mesozoic stratigraphic boundary, there is no known deposit of extraterrestrial platinum-group metals, nor is there any other form of evidence of an asteroid impact. Flood basalts, though, occurred right then, covering roughly a million square miles of Siberia to depths exceeding twelve thousand feet. In the mid-nineteen-eighties, the geophysicist W. Jason Morgan, whose work on geophysical hot spots has been regarded by some as an even larger contribution to the advancement of science than his revelation, in the nineteen-sixties, of the basic geometries of plate tectonics, reacted to the asteroid hypothesis by noting that a skein of mass extinctions (including the Cretaceous and Permian Extinctions) coincide with the initiation of hot spots. Flood basalts in the Central Atlantic, for example, mark the end of Triassic time.

Meanwhile, not a few paleontologists interpret the fossil record in a light that deëmphasizes both the Yucatán catastrophe and, to a lesser extent, the flood basalts. The paleontologists take such things into full account, but what they assemble from the evidence in the rock is a laminated story, far less clear and far more complex. In a 2005 paper in the *Australian Journal of Earth Sciences*, the Princeton paleontologist Gerta Keller mentions depletions of ocean oxygen, global warming, and pronounced rises of sea level among the developments that have prefigured mass extinctions, whether volcanism and asteroidal impact were or were not involved. In a paper published in 2001 in *Planetary and Space Science*, Keller says of the Yucatán asteroid, "This theory unquestionably has great sex appeal. The largest and most fascinating creatures that ever roamed the Earth were wiped out in a single day in a ball of fire caused by a meteorite impact that leaves behind the crater of doom. . . . The existence of an impact crater alone, however, neither proves nor explains the demise of the dinosaurs, or the mass extinction of any other groups." In the words of Monica Wojcik, recently one of Keller's students, "Essentially she sees the end-Cretaceous as what she calls 'the bad-luck theory'—a bunch of natural events piling up at once." Add to the equation continental drift, atmospheric carbon dioxide, and glaciation, among other things. Climate has been severely altered as continents have changed position, not only in latitude but also with respect to one another. In the late Ordovician, for example, as three ancestral continents coalesced on their way to becoming the northern part of Pangaea, there was about ten times as much atmospheric carbon dioxide as there is today, large parts of the landmass were thickly covered with ice, and the period ended with a two-phase mass extinction that is thought by some paleontologists to have been even deadlier than the Cretaceous Extinction. "In this case," Keller says, "all fingers point toward glaciation" as the leading cause. "Glaciation causes turnover. Cool water brings toxic things up from black shale." The Ordovician ocean became anoxic. When the dying occurred, there were no bolides peppering the earth and no fresh flood basalts anywhere.

It's enough to ruffle conventional wisdom, unsettling the jury as to who killed whom, and what killed what. While the earth moves on toward the first mass extinction caused by a living species, debates about earlier ones are really unresolved.

Loose on the Downs with Harry:

The top leadership of MI5 was an inverted T—one over

one over five. Doyne-Ditmas was among the five. And now he's twice retired and at large atop the chalk cliffs, coolly walking the fenceless lip in rain driven by forty-mile winds, his white hair streaming. When he was nineteen, in Massachusetts, he was Lord Mountararat in "Iolanthe." Now he is Hal Doyne-Lear on the chalky bourn—Gloucester with eyes. He says it is "raining stair rods." What a peculiar expression, methinks. Stair rods hold carpets to stairs, while dogs and cats gauge rain. These are the white cliffs of Sussex—Cuckmere Haven to Beachy Head—the whitest in the Cretaceous Terrain, fairly glaring in the sun when there's a sun. Eroded in a rhythm of reëntrants and promontories, they call to mind a row of clerestory windows. Almost straight down them—hundreds of feet—are waves. Hal holds his camera over the edge. After MI5 and elsewhere in government, he took the name Harry and halved his professional surname to become Harry Ditmas. Behind us, the view north is of a vast deep swale and then the rising hills, cattle far up there like chocolate bits. Looking for something as original as the stair rods, I ask Harry what sorts of words the English choose to describe their remarkable downlands. He says, " 'Rolling' comes along rather quickly." To the east is Beachy Head, the highest, giddiest chalk cliff in Britain, where the Upper Chalk emerges from the English Channel to become the South Downs. "God is always greater than all of our troubles," says a small plaque a few yards from the edge. And a sign: "The Samaritans—Always There, Day or Night, 735555 or 08457 909090."

Chalk is calcium carbonate. Limestone is calcium carbonate. Why these cliffs are chalk and not limestone is a matter of ocean chemistry, of whether the mineral vestiges of planktonic life, settling on the seafloor as oozes and muds, needed to recrystallize as limestone or could indurate in their original texture. Pure calcium carbonate—$CaCO_3$—can vary in mineral structure. The word for such differing forms is "polymorph." Diamonds and graphite, both of which are pure carbon, are the world's most renowned polymorphs. Aragonite and calcite, mineral forms of $CaCO_3$, were the first polymorphs described in the history of chemistry. Aragonite is unstable and needs to recrystallize as limestone, while pure calcite is content to be chalk. In Phanerozoic time—a term that embraces the five hundred and forty-four million years before the present—the ocean has alternately been a calcite ocean and an aragonite ocean, changing three times. It was a calcite ocean when the white cliffs formed. It's an aragonite ocean now. Limestone, slowly, is soluble in water (those caverns and caves), but it is also hard and impermeable (the Empire State Building). Chalk is soft and porous. The Chunnel goes through chalk. Le Souterrain Crétacé. When the Chunnel opened, in 1994, the Department of Transport's director and coordinator of transport security—responsible for the security of everything that rolled, flew, or floated in the United Kingdom—was Harry.

His full actual name is Harold Granville Terence Payne Doyne-Ditmas. Whatever he is called, I have a question for him: How fast are these cliffs eroding? Alone one morning on the Undercliff Coastal Walk, near Ovingdean on the way to Rottingdean, I picked up a hunk of chalk the size of a rugby ball that had just fallen from above, its fresh broken facets pearl-white. Chalk rains on the pavement of the Undercliff Coastal Walk, and breaks down underfoot, turning into pewter mud (lime ooze) and recapitulating its history. Signs everywhere: "Do not use the Undercliff in bad weather. The sea and sea defences can be hazardous. Falls of chalk and flint can occur without warning."

"Keep off the groynes." Doyne-Ditmas reminds me that erosion rates are not among his preoccupations. He answers my question empirically, though, driving to the water's edge at Birling Gap and stopping before a coast-guard barracks that, like a motel, is a long narrow terrace, a set of attached "cottages." The building's axis, running north-south, is ninety degrees to the line of the beach, which, for miles on either side, is also the line of the cliffs. Dating from the nineteenth century, the coast-guard barracks were built symmetrically, their beachward and landward arms meeting in a central unit of somewhat different proportion. But one arm now is a good bit shorter than the other. The once central unit is eccentric. The end that reaches toward the sea has been, in effect, lopped off by the sea. In a chalk boulder field near the building, some of the fallen boulders are ten feet in diameter. A lighthouse up the cliff was recently moved back seventeen metres, to keep it from falling with the chalk. The cliffs of Sussex are being eroded, we learn, at an average rate of about thirty-five centimetres a year. Thus, in forty thousand years the Downs will be down to the elevation of the Weald, and in a couple of hundred thousand more the cliffs now at Dover will be standing in London or Gravesend or Chalk. Sounds slow, but geomorphologically that is fast. Nowhere near as fast, however, as the excavation of the English Channel. The two most relevant masses of ice that covered northwestern Europe in late Pleistocene time were the Fennoscandian Ice Sheet and the British Ice Sheet. The latter, a mile thick, covered most of Ireland, all of Scotland, all of Wales, and England south to a line more or less between Cambridge and Oxford. With ice on North America and so much of Europe, sea level was some four hundred feet lower than it is at present. The Thames Valley was not glaciated, and the Thames flowed out into a larger river, known in geology as the Channel River, which ran between England and France through dry land bedrocked with chalk. When the ice melted, the meltwaters turned the Thames into a hydroplow and the Channel River into a cold Amazon, fed also by the Rhine, the Maas, the Somme, and the Seine, and from Scandinavia as well. This was the greatest river system that has ever drained Europe, and without much resistance it gouged out the English Channel and drove back to the two sides the chalk cliffs of France and England. Erosion rated, Harry pauses at a blackthorn to collect a pocketful of sloes for his next batch of sloe gin. Jackdaws, peregrines, kittiwakes, and kestrels are overhead. Sloes are like hard blue grapes.

In Hal's early years in the Box, he sat for a time at a desk next to David Cornwell, an exact contemporary who left the service to extend his career as John le Carré. Hal served abroad at times—in Kuala Lumpur, for example, and in Moscow, where his cover job at the British Embassy was "line manager of a hundred local staff, all, presumably at least, co-opted workers of the K.G.B." As he went to bed in Moscow each night, he imagined that if he were to speak aloud in a dream the K.G.B. would be recording what he said. He served in Belfast in the nineteen-eighties. A night came when he and his wife, Julia, "had to do a rapid moonlight flit," leaving their house "permanently and forever," after it was realized that his cover was blown. In Eastbourne, under Beachy Head, he shows me the prep school from which he was evacuated during the Second World War. Like the Normans at Hastings, which is ten miles from Eastbourne, the Wehrmacht intended to invade this coastline. Loose on the Downs, I keep thinking of those cattle nearly infinitesimal far up the rolling grasslands, and remembering that in his prime Harry could have picked one off. While the rest of us were playing rugger, squash, tennis, or basketball, Harry was firing rifles at extremely distant targets. His public school, Uppingham, had been by his literal description "far and away the most successful shooting school." He had competed in Britain and Canada as one of the Cambridge VIII, and after Cambridge he went global on British national teams. I went out to a range with him once in those years, near Woking, in Surrey, on the chalk of the North Downs. We looked far across the coalescing hills at targets smaller than cows. Gratuitously, Hal observed that his sport was not played with a moving ball you could dribble. As he describes it now, success or failure depended on "ability to judge the wind, and not being nervous; being able to concentrate; not to panic when the pressure is on." Golf with gunpowder. The bull's-eye was twenty-four inches wide. "You might have to allow for twenty-five feet of drift at a thousand yards. We used ordinary Army-issue .303 rifles, essentially unimproved." On a wall at his home in Brighton are two antique nineteenth-century rifles— one from each side at Tel-el-Kebir. His grandfather Edward Ditmas brought them home.

Close up, the chalk cliffs appear to be studded, almost like formal shirts, with uniform black dots. They line up in horizontal rows. Spaces are even from dot to dot and also between rows, which are about a metre apart. The impression given is of bedding planes, but those horizontal rows are not bedding planes. Sponge spicules and other forms of organic silicon were among the impurities in the original chalk deposit. Within a given and consistent cubic dimension of chalk, the contained silicon dioxide will gather itself until it forms a very dense silicon-dioxide nodule, which is also known as cryptocrystalline quartz. Like chert, agate, jasper, and chalcedony, flint is cryptocrystalline quartz. Those black dots in the chalk cliffs are chunks of flint. The shingle beaches below the white cliffs consist almost entirely of flint cobbles the size of ostrich eggs. If you stand next to a chalk cliff and lift your head, you look up a wall spiky with projecting flints. When they fall, they sometimes break. A cracked-open surface, opaque and light to dark gray, is smooth and shines like glass. The old structures of half of Sussex, not to mention Surrey, seem to be made of flint—flint churches, flint terraces, flint houses reinforced with bricks at the corners, flint retaining walls bordering sunken lanes. Doyne-Ditmas seems especially fond of the big flint prison in Lewes, its flints, black and gray, "giving it a sort of piebald aspect." In some flint construction, the nodules were left whole. More often, they were hammered open—cracked like walnuts—so that their flat glassy surfaces would shine. The process is known as knapping and the results are knapped flints. Some flints were knapped so painstakingly that their outer surfaces were not only flat but also rectangular. In building walls they seem to be obsidian bricks.

Parting glimpses of the chalk:

In Downe, on the North Downs, in Charles Darwin's Down House, is a portrait in chalk of Darwin's wife, Emma. A billiard table is on display, no lack of chalk for the cues. Darwin did all his great work in this place, where he lived after the Beagle for the rest of his life. He and Emma had ten children. Darwin played a lot of billiards, possibly to get away from the children but certainly, as he wrote in a letter, because "it does me a deal of good, and drives the horrid species out of my head." His garden walls are panels of stratified flint. If you drive here from, say, the north side of the Thames, you move very slowly from stoplight to stoplight through the heavy density of South London, scarcely a patch of green, and then, suddenly, you're in Darwin's Downe, on swelling land among pony carts and open fields, horses, jodhpurred women perched in saddles, knapped flints like oyster shells up the wall of a country teahouse called Evolution 1.

Flints from English chalk ignited the powder that answered the shot heard round the world.

Flints from English chalk ignited the muskets that broke the Scottish clans.

Chalk is the bedrock of Salisbury Plain, so the stones of Stonehenge came from as far away as Wales.

Romans on the English chalk built roadbeds of flint cobbles and covered them with compacted gravel and slag.

One Roman road ran close by the White Horse of Uffington, if the white horse was—as it is claimed to be—already there. Scraped into the chalk of a steep hill in the Berkshire Downs, the white horse is three hundred and seventy-four feet long.

The Long Man of Wilmington, scraped into the chalk of the South Downs escarpment—his date of origin unknown—is two hundred and thirty-five feet tall.

The Cerne Abbas Giant, on a bald hill in Dorset, is a chalk figure a hundred and eighty feet tall, also known as the Rude Man. His penis is erect and thirty feet long. His testicles are ten feet wide. English couples ascend the hill, lie down on the giant, and couple. Women who wish to conceive spend a night alone on the penis.

The storied streams of Hampshire run in their fecundity over Upper Cretaceous chalk. In Newton Stacey, where the Dever meets the Test, you walk down to the confluence as if circling a room from one Constable landscape to the next—passing through hedgerowed fields and under horse chestnuts, opening and shutting gates, "BEWARE THE BULL." Coot are swimming on the River Test, two swans and four cygnets on the Dever. Over the junction pool, an ash ripe with ash keys spreads its canopy across the two rivers. They are surprisingly narrow and intimate, not much more than brooks—the Test, the mother stream, scarcely three feet deep and thirty wide. Its bank, squared off and shored with planking, is level and closely mowed so that anglers can walk beside the water unimpeded, dry shod, with no thought of stepping in. It just isn't done, stepping in. The air is full of damselflies, midges, mayflies, swifts, and swallows, the sandy chalky bottom thick with cress and water crowfoot. The angler is wise to creep along the footpath, or, at least, to tiptoe. One unwary step and a two-pound brown explodes from cover under the lip of the bank and vanishes upstream. You sit down on a bench and think it over. Arctic grayling, which have even higher standards of water quality than trout do, share this sacred water, as does *Esox lucius*— the piscivorous Devil, the savage Fiend, the pike—known to grow as large as one stone three consuming trout. The underwater water crowfoot grows so fast that the waterkeeper mows it like the grass. In his fish garden, beside the Dever, the waterkeeper's shed roofs are thatched, a bull trout is memorialized that was "killed August 1934," and drying at the tops of posts are the heads of four huge pike.

SWIMMING WITH CANOES

I grew up in a summer camp—Keewaydin—whose specialty was canoes and canoe travel. At the home base, near Middlebury, Vermont, were racks and racks of canoes, at least a hundred canoes—E. M. Whites and Chestnuts, mainly. They were very good wood-and-canvas keeled or keelless canoes, lake or river canoes. We were in them every day wherever we were, in and out of Vermont. We were like some sort of crustaceans with our rib-and-planking exoskeletons, and to this day I do not feel complete or safe unless I am surrounded by the protective shape of a canoe.

Now and again, Keewaydin let us take our canoes not so much onto the water as into it, during swim period. We went swimming with our canoes. We jounced. Jouncing is the art of propelling a canoe without a paddle. You stand up on the gunwales near the stern deck and repeatedly flex and unflex your knees. The canoe rocks, slaps the lake, moves forward. Sooner or later, you lose your balance and fall into the water, because the gunwales are slender rails and the stern deck is somewhat smaller than a pennant. From waters deeper than you were tall, you climbed back into your canoe. If you think that's easy, try it.

After three or four splats, and with a belly pink from hauling it over gunwales, you lost interest in jouncing. What next? You sat in your canoe and deliberately overturned it. You leaned hard to one side, grabbed the opposite gunwale, and pulled. Out you went and into the water. This was, after all, swim period. Now you rolled your canoe, an action it resists far less when it is loaded with water. You could make your canoe spiral like a football inside the lake.

And before long you found the air pocket. Having jounced and spiralled to the far end of your invention span, you ducked beneath the surface and swam in under your upside-down canoe. You rose slowly to miss a thwart—feeling above you, avoiding a bump on the head—and then your eyes, nose, mouth were in air, among chain-link streaks of white and amber light, the shimmers of reflection in a Quonset grotto. Its vertical inches were few but enough. Your pals got in there with you and your voices were tympanic in the grotto. Or you just hung out under there by yourself. With a hand on a thwart, and your feet slowly kicking, you could breathe normally, see normally, talk abnormally, and wait indefinitely for a change of mood. You were invisible to the upside, outside world. Even more than when kneeling in a fast current, you were one with your canoe.

Kneeling in a fast current. Once in a while, we went to what is now called Battell Gorge, north of Middlebury, to learn to deal with really fast, pounding, concentrated flow. Otter Creek, there, undergoes an abrupt change in physiographic character. After meandering benignly through the marshes, woodlots, and meadows of the Champlain Valley, it encounters a large limestone outcrop, which it deeply bisects. By a factor of three or four, the stream narrows and the water squeezes into humps, haystacks, souse holes, and standing waves, as it drops ten feet in a hundred yards. Then it emerges from the high limestone walls and the darkness of overhanging hemlocks into the light of a pool so wide it seems to be a pond.

Like horse people, we showed up some distance above the head of the gorge with trailers—racked trailers that each carried seven canoes. The gorge was a good place to learn how to deal with them in white water because it was violent but short. In that narrow, roaring flume, you didn't have to choose the best route— didn't have to look for what the *voyageurs* called the *fil d'eau*. There was pretty much one way to go. But you got the sense of a canoe flying in three dimensions; and the more you did it the slower it seemed, the shoot separating itself into distinct parts, as if you were in a balloon rising in sunlight and falling in the shadows of clouds.

One time, when I was about twelve, I went into the gorge in a very old canoe that was missing its stern seat. (We didn't take the better boats there.) Two of us were paddling it. I was kneeling against the stern thwart, which was so far back it was only eight or ten inches from gunwale to gunwale, the size of my young butt. My right knee was on the canoe's ribs, and my right leg extended so far back that my foot was wedged in the V of the stern when the bucking canoe turned over. Billy Furey was my partner, and we were doing all we could to keep things even, but whatever we did wasn't good enough and we flipped near the top of the gorge. Billy was ejected. Among the countless wonders of the simple design of the native American canoe is the fact that it ejects its paddlers when it capsizes.

This one could not eject me, because my foot was stuck. I struggled to pull the foot free, but it wouldn't come. Upside down in billows of water, I could not get out. Understand: I have

a lifelong tendency to panic. Almost anything will panic me—
health, money, working with words. Almost anything—I'm here
to tell you—but an overturned canoe in a raging gorge. When I
was trapped in there, if panic crossed my mind it went out the
other side. I had, after all, time and time again been swimming
with canoes. There was purpose in letting us do that—a thought
that had never occurred to me. After I realized I was caught and
was not going to be coming out from under that canoe, I reached
for the stern quarter-thwart, took hold of it, and pulled my body
upward until my eyes, nose, and mouth were in the grotto. There,
in the dancing light, I rode on through the gorge, and when the
water calmed down at the far end I gave the canoe half a spiral
and returned to the open sunlight.

WARMING THE JUMP SEAT

Mr. Boyden liked to say—at evening meeting in the Old Dorm before the first game, for example—that the smallest player on his basketball team was shorter than he was. Mr. Boyden was the coach. I was the player. From an elevation of five feet seven inches, I towered over him.

As a coach, he was, in other ways as well, a romantic. He was all O's and no X's, with a concentrated surge of spirit. A reverse pivot or a back-door play would have been too deceptive. He once took me out of a game, sourly said, "That's high-school stuff," and then immediately put me back in.

I go into all this to suggest the origins of the book I was to write about him seventeen years later. It began in the gym and on the road trips with the man we never but never addressed or referred to as "Coach." In addition to coaching football, basketball, and baseball, Frank L. Boyden was the headmaster of the school.

As it happened, I was public-high-school stuff in fact as well as behavior. I was a graduate of Princeton High School, in New Jersey, and a deferred admittee to Princeton University. Deerfield Academy was my mother's idea. Before I went to college, she wanted me out of town and more mature.

I had loved high school and high-school basketball, and refused to leave any of it prematurely. In comparison, Deerfield was—to understate the case—novel. Attendance was taken exactly seventeen times a day. You surely had a sense that you belonged. In all kinds of ways, actually, the school was abundantly welcoming, and soon made this new-boy senior feel as if he'd been a part of it for the three previous years. In fall, attendance was taken on the Lower Level playing fields by Robert McGlynn with a clipboard. Relying on recognition alone, he checked off names. In the ranks and files of lightweight-football calisthenics, he failed to see me. He walked around behind my jumping and flapping teammates, and found me lying on the ground looking at the sky. He liked that. He checked me off. In the extended indolence on the grass, he recognized essence of writer. Mr. McGlynn was an English teacher who did not know a forward pass from a set shot. He gave me books to read, and talked about them with me in an informal way. I wasn't even in his class. We would be friends for forty-some years, for the rest of his life.

Fortunately, Mr. Boyden had Larry Bohrer, a chemistry teacher, as his basketball-coaching assistant. Mr. Bohrer literally studied the game in books until he could address its most common situations as if they were chemical reactions. He figured things out so well that we beat a couple of teams that had better players.

We travelled all over New England in two elongate Cadillacs, one for Mr. Bohrer and the second five, one for Mr. Boyden and the first five. Foster L. Babineau was the starting chauffeur. One player rode up front with him, and Mr. Boyden made sure that the three tallest players sat on the back seat, where their legs had ample room to stretch. Mr. Boyden always consigned the two minutest people to the little fold-out jump seats—himself and me. To Ashburnham and Wilbraham, Wallingford and Saxtons

River—Massachusetts, Connecticut, and Vermont—he and I rode side by side through the frozen country. When he was awake, we talked. The length of the car was conducive to three conversations, and ours was the one in the middle. He had almost nothing to say about basketball beyond a few remarks about the coming game. He talked about his school. There was never a need to ask him to do that. For my part, because I had come from a public high school, I was especially interested in what made Deerfield work, and what made Deerfield work was sitting on the other jump seat.

In 1965, encouraged by McGlynn and prodded into action by my first geology mentor, Frank Conklin, I undertook to attempt to write a profile of Mr. Boyden for *The New Yorker*, where, in those days, pieces of writing found their own appropriate dimensions, and ranged in length from haiku to book. Mr. Boyden grumpily acquiesced, and I spent a large part of that autumn living in a far back room in his extended house. He was beginning his sixty-fourth year as Deerfield's headmaster, and even the outer lenses of his horizon included no plans whatever for retirement. He sometimes talked about retirement, but talk was the sum of the topic for him. This day and that, we were back on the road, Foster L. Babineau still at the wheel. Mr. Boyden took me to Boston to meet a man quite close to him in age who had retired nearly twenty years before as headmaster of Exeter (Lewis Perry), and an Amherst classmate, Robert Maynard, aged about eighty-five, at his desk in downtown Boston, chairman of R. H. Stearns. On the way back to Deerfield after dark, our tank was low on gas and we stopped to fill it. Scarce had the pump finished pumping when the gas station and everything around it went dark. As we proceeded west, whole towns would go black as we were passing through. We were experiencing the great power blackout of 1965, when, in domino fashion, a large part of the northeastern grid totally lost it. Babineau and I, at any rate, were experiencing the blackout. As town after town pitched dark around us, I doubt that the headmaster was aware of it. He was too intent to notice a power blackout, whatever its size. He was talking about his school.

Before I left Deerfield to write the profile, the headmaster's wife, Mrs. Helen Boyden, in whose classroom I had sat learning chemistry, took me aside to offer me additional instruction. She said, "Whatever you do, do not show the manuscript to the headmaster." Her son John, who was the school's director of admissions, had already taken me aside to say, "Whatever you do, don't show him the manuscript before you publish it." I wasn't born in that blackout. I assured them both that I understood what they were saying. I appreciated their insight and support.

The profile was published in two issues of the magazine. When the first part appeared, the headmaster happened to be in Los Angeles for a Deerfield gathering. John Boyden was there, too, and later described to me the following scene: The headmaster, in a hotel room, picked up *The New Yorker*. He read it for a time, and then stood up and sent *The New Yorker* flying through the air and into a wall. It fell behind a couch. Time passed. Eventually, he reached down behind the couch and retrieved the magazine. He read for a time. Then he sent it fluttering into another wall. Soon he picked it up, read a little more, and flung it again.

While his wife and son had articulated what amounts to a journalistic principle, there was, of course, no way in the world to prevent the headmaster from seeing the material before it was reprinted as a book. Having heard the Los Angeles story from

John Boyden, I had no idea what to expect, but a very clear idea that I could expect something. It came in the form of a genial invitation. Please come to Deerfield and go over the text.

What to do? I felt dread. I thought I'd be taken out of the game. "That's high-school stuff." I went.

I found him in the front room of his house enjoying a steaming cup of hot water. He was looking through a neatly assembled, hand-made book that consisted of cut-out *New Yorker* columns absolved from their flanking ads and mounted on white paper. As we turned the pages, sitting side by side on two small chairs, he was amiable, anecdotal, and matter-of-fact. Wherever there was something that troubled him, he stopped to tell me what it was. He stopped nowhere near as often as I had thought he would. He told me he had no desire to diminish my piece of writing but there were some things he wanted me to understand. One at a time, without hurry, he went through them. I was tense all the way, but then, at the end, felt suddenly relaxed. After I went home, I changed some things and left others as they had been. From beginning to end, the points he had raised had to do with others—with the sensitivities of townspeople, teachers, and students, and of their families and descendants. Not one of his objections had to do with himself.

SPIN RIGHT AND
SHOOT LEFT

You're on defense, zone defense. You pick up a loose ball and look for the outlet pass. You see it, throw it, and go down the middle on a fast break, taking the return pass. Now you're looking for a three-on-two or a two-on-one before they can set up their defense. Too late, they're settled—man-to-man. You're still looking for a two-on-one, but it's more complicated. You see and sense everybody—where they are, where they're headed, as things develop in almost constant motion. You watch for a backdoor cut, and for someone posting up. Maybe go for an outside shot. The coach is yelling his mantra, "Look for the open man!" There is no open man. Wary of a double-team, you give up the ball with a bounce pass. One player to the next, the ball moves two, three, four times before you set a pick, roll, take a no-look pass, and go to the hoop for a layup. Are you playing basketball? No.

You could be, of course, every term and move alike. But this is lacrosse, which is essentially the same game—an assertion that loses a good deal of its novelty in the light of the fact that James Naismith, best known for inventing basketball, in 1891, and writing and publishing basketball's original rules, in 1892, was a lacrosse player. A Canadian, he had played lacrosse in the eighteen-eighties at McGill, and also for the New York Lacrosse Club.

Lacrosse and basketball are siblings of soccer, hockey, and water polo. When the rules of ice hockey were written, in the eighteen-seventies, a model they followed was lacrosse. The transfer of lacrosse from Iroquoian to European culture had occurred in Montreal in mid-century, and while the white sport was to emigrate and develop most emphatically in the eastern United States, Canadians would retain it strongly here and there—"here" being southeastern Ontario, "there" consisting of some great leaps over territory unfamiliar in the game. Paul and Gary Gait, twins who played for Syracuse (1987–90) and who constitute in themselves a hall of fame within the Hall of Fame, grew up in Victoria, British Columbia, a hotbed of lacrosse. David Mitchell, Cornell '07, a prestidigitational stickhandler who plays in both professional lacrosse leagues (indoor and outdoor), grew up and went to high school in Moose Jaw, Saskatchewan. Wayne Gretzky, ice hockey's historically greatest star, grew up in Brantford, Ontario. As winters wore on, Gretzky has said, "I could hardly wait to get my lacrosse stick out and start throwing the ball around. It didn't matter how cold or rainy it would be, we'd be out firing the ball against walls and working on our moves."

In lacrosse as in hockey, Gretzky was at home in the power play, also known as "man-up" and "e.m.o."—the extra-man opportunity that results when somebody is sent out of the game for a time as a result of a violation, such as "slashing," an unambiguous term common to hockey and lacrosse. Hockey's power play is still a bit rough-hewn—for example, one player, in close, acting as a screen, the others stitching around him a silhouette of slap shots—and in evolutionary terms has not progressed nearly as far as the fast-weaving passes of lacrosse, which gradually tease apart an open man. Water polo—whose fakes and shots will translate into the other games—uses the e.m.o. to punish various torts, like taking your opponent to the bottom of the pool. In lacrosse, advancing the ball from one end of the field to the other is known as clearing, and the defensive attempt to stop the clear is known as riding. Soccer coaches have said that soccer consists of lacrosse's clearing and riding. The basketball term for riding is "full-court press." The most difficult pass in lacrosse traverses the field from one side to the other while both players are running. Soccer calls that a square ball. Of these five games—with their picks and screens, their fast breaks and rotational defenses, their high degree of continuous motion—water polo, in its sluggish medium, is surely the most awkward, and lacrosse, at the other extreme, creates the fastest and crispest accumulation of passes and is the prettiest to watch.

Four of these sports are played in the Olympics. The other is lacrosse. There is a Bulgarian Lacrosse Federation, a Korean Lacrosse Association, a Deutscher Lacrosse Verband, an Öster-reichischer Lacrosse Verband, a Nederlandse Lacrosse Bond, a Suomen Lacrosseliitto ry, Lacrosse Polska, Schweiz Lacrosse, and similar organizations in Spain, Hong Kong, Latvia, Australia, New Zealand, Argentina, Canada, Sweden, Denmark, Bermuda, Scotland, Ireland, England, Italy, Slovakia, Slovenia, the Czech Republic. A few years ago, the Princeton lacrosse team finished its season by touring Japan, because there were fifteen thousand lacrosse players in Japan. To the Japanese, a visiting Division I American lacrosse team was an educational opportunity. Near the end of the visit, Princeton was asked to play, against assorted Japanese teams, eight complete lacrosse games in one day. Bill Tierney, Princeton's coach, was uncharacteristically at a loss for words. Like American football teams, lacrosse teams usually play once a week and need the time to recover. Holding up a pair of fingers, Tierney said, "Two."

As lacrosse has spread to East Asia, East Asia has entered the cerebral cortex of lacrosse. Dave Pietramala, the head coach at the Johns Hopkins University, has studied Sun Tzu on military strategy. Sun Tzu dates from twenty-five centuries ago, in the time of Aristotle and Alexander the Great. After reading Sun Tzu on deception ("All warfare is based on deception"), Pietramala looked more favorably than ever on the Hopkins defensive fake slide. Like his ancient mentor, Pietramala preaches patience. Sun Tzu: "If it is to your advantage to make a forward move, make a forward move; if not, stay where you are." Hopkins has won nine N.C.A.A. championships since the N.C.A.A. began its tournaments, in 1971. (Before then, national champions were declared.) Pietramala achieved his first in 2005. In 1928, in a premature attempt to sell lacrosse to the Olympics, Major General Douglas MacArthur, the president of the American Olympic Committee, organized a lacrosse tournament to determine what American team would demonstrate lacrosse in matches against Great Britain and Canada at the summer Games in Amsterdam. Hopkins defeated Maryland for the honor.

The International Federation of Women's Lacrosse Associations has held a World Cup tournament every four years since 1982. The first was in Nottingham. The latest was in Annapolis, Maryland (Australia 14, U.S. 7), to be followed by Prague. Men's World Lacrosse Championships have been held every four years since 1974, most recently in London, Ontario, where Team U.S.A., which had won the tournament seven of nine times, got past the Iroquois, 21–13, but lost in the final to Canada. The populationally outnumbered Iroquois hold their own in these tournaments, usually finishing well up in the column. They travel on Iroquois passports. They do not seek membership in the Indian National Lacrosse Federation. At a bar in Dublin late last spring, a manager of the English national men's lacrosse team remarked that some Iroquois have two sets of sticks, modern ones and old "woodies," "and man do they hurt when they check with them." He said, "They really do hold their own as a lacrosse nation." In 2006, after narrowly beating England, "they took the Australians apart; they bring something special to every World Championship—they are the life and soul of our sport."

I was in Dublin with the Princeton men's lacrosse team, of which I am a Faculty Fellow (an official position, not unlike shaman, that was thought up some years ago by the university's athletic director, Gary Walters, who can think up just about anything). Earlier, we had been in southeastern Spain, near Cartagena, at a high-rent sporting club called La Manga, where Spanish Open golf tournaments have been played, where a tennis stadium is surrounded by twenty-seven outside courts, and where a spread of cricket pitches and no fewer than eight state-of-the-art soccer fields have attracted cricketers and footballers of the highest level. Manchester United warms up there. Princeton—scheduled to play two games on consecutive days against the English national lacrosse team—arrived on the eve of the first match after a long bus ride to J.F.K. that included streets of midtown Manhattan, a night flight to Dublin, a 6 A.M. departure for Alicante, which is as close to Dublin as New York is to Minneapolis, and, finally, an hour's bus ride from Alicante to La Manga, where the team arrived with ample time to change into their uniforms, get into other buses, and ride to a field to practice. Goals, grass, sidelines, restraining boxes, end lines, creases—everything was perfect, and perfectly marked. Bill Tierney ran his team for two hours. They didn't seem at all sleepless, and he finished them off with wind sprints. Then he called them together for a word: This was no Roman holiday; these were games of importance to international lacrosse, and they were to play with finesse, not flash, proving how well they could play, not how showily. Looking around, he didn't need to add: No behind-the-back passes, no behind-the-back-hot-dog shots at the English goalie. Since they apparently thought sleep was what other people do, he told them to make curfew, and he would be around to see that they did. "Give this team a good game," he said. "They have better sticks than we do."

What that meant was that the English would pass, catch, shoot, scoop, and cradle with more stickhandling skill than their American opponents. Really? Really. In the first game, an English midfielder, sprinting up his left sideline to take a pass on a clear, looked over his shoulder and saw that the ball was headed wide, low, and out of bounds. Without breaking stride, and keeping his feet always inches inbounds, he extended his left arm and lacrosse stick far over the sideline, lowered the head almost to the ground, and turned the pocket backward. Seven feet from the player's shoulder, six inches above the ground, the ball went into the pocket, then, still running full tilt, the English midfielder flipped the head of the stick and brought it up into shooting position as he veered toward the Princeton goal.

A lacrosse stick is a rigid slingshot. American toddlers learn to handle lacrosse sticks in certain locations more than in others—notably, in Baltimore. Manchester has been called "the Baltimore of English lacrosse." The Mancunian press has called Baltimore the Manchester of the United States. That English midfielder was a Mancunian. Some seventy-five per cent of English lacrosse players are natives of Greater Manchester. Men's world championships have been held in Manchester. In the eighteen-nineties, at the British lacrosse championship, a Mancunian donated a trophy for the winner, calling it the Iroquois Cup.

After the lacrosse games in Spain and a third game a few days later against England in Ireland—after the Princeton players got into their buses and went back to their rooms—Bill Tierney stayed on, at the request of the English nationals, to conduct clinics for the English players. It being his opinion that they were long on stickhandling and short on strategy, he told them that they expended too much energy "running east-west and not enough running north-south." He told them he was "seeing a lot of green down the middle, down that alley," and they were not taking advantage of it. "When you dodge and run, head to the far pipe. Going for the far corner of the pipe is a mental idea." He talked volubly, rapidly, with the absence of hesitation of someone completely grounded in his subject, and he showed no concern for his American accent; he was speaking lacrosse. If he mentioned isos, they understood that he meant isododging—one against one. "North-south" is parallel to sidelines, "east-west" is parallel to end lines. You don't accomplish much running east-west; you attack by running north-south.

"The guy who makes the play is often not the guy who got the assist or the goal. It starts two or three passes earlier. We all get the goal."

"Lacrosse is essentially a matter of looking for a two-on-one. You get it by dodging, passing, or picking."

"If you hear the word 'switch,' put your shoulder in it and go for the goal."

"Get outside your comfort zone—go left."

"Number 40, you used your shot fake enough times to make it ineffective. Use it when it counts."

Tierney himself seemed to have been trained in some sort of diplomatic clinic. He had many genuine compliments for the English players, seasoned with deprecations of his own players (who weren't there). On the craft of scoring, he said, "You shoot to the opposite knee." On the art of precision shooting, he said, "If my guys could hit the corners, I would tell them to shoot there. But I tell them to shoot for the knees or the shoulders. Then they'll hit the corners." (He has had players who could hit a falling leaf.)

"If you shoot from square, you can't get everything on it that you want." (When you shoot from square, a line drawn between your feet would be perpendicular to the direction of your shot.)

"Do your inside roll. Feel the pressure of the defense."

"Do the rocker step, come back up top."

"Split hard to his top foot." (Make your dodge and pass the defender on the side where his foot is more advanced.)

"That's about as far as you are going to get to go before they double you."

Setting up drill lines for two-on-twos, he taught them a pick-and-roll variation that he called Kodiak, because Princeton invented it for a game against Brown. It was reminiscent of the confined space, tight maneuvering, and superb stickhandling of Iroquois and Canadian indoor lacrosse, transposed by Tierney to the outdoor game. Occurring topside (in front of the goal), it could result in various achievements, such as causing a long-stick defenseman (a "pole") to be replaced by a defender with a short stick, or producing a maneuver resulting in a score; set the pick, and after the roll "make that little Kodiak-type pass, over the shoulder."

Both figuratively and literally, the most exploitable dimension in the game of lacrosse is the more than eight thousand square feet of playing space behind each goal, the focus of which is an area known as X. Tierney mentioned various dodges crafted for coming out of X, the simplest of which was pure speed—the "speed dodge," the "rush dodge," the "bull dodge."

"You just sprint to get topside. Gauge your defenseman. If he can't run with you, you're going to beat him all day." (Defensemen, who were once burly and slow, have become burly and fast—or especially adroit at changing direction.) "Don't run curving routes. Make sure that whatever you can do is in straight lines. Sprint to seven and seven." The numbers refer to a topside locale called the island—seven yards wide of the goal and seven yards in front of it. What to do on the island? "You have four options: Turn and shoot with your opposite hand; for example, spin right and shoot left-handed. Split and go under. Plant, and inside roll. Rocker step, then shoot from topside." The English faces suggested nothing short of complete comprehension until Tierney added, "Five and five is what you really want when you say seven and seven. It's like saying the curfew is at 1 A.M. and they get in at three."

In Dublin, most went to the Guinness brewery, some visited the Book of Kells, and I missed the bus to the lacrosse game. One moment, two buses were waiting—at Jurys Inn Christchurch—

and the lobby was a sea of orange-and-black equipment bags and uniformed players. I went up to my room for something I had forgotten, and when I returned the lobby was vacant and the buses were gone. I had nothing on paper that said where the game was to be, and I don't text-message anybody. The *Irish Times* did not know where the game was. The *Irish Times* does not know lacrosse from camogie or hurling. I went to the front desk and asked the clerk where the buses had gone. She was an intern from China, and she did not understand me. She said this was her first full day in Ireland. I asked a male clerk. No comprehension (Bucharest). I consulted my cash position. Two euros. But money was the least of my problems; I knew nowhere to go.

Into the rising panic, three remembered letters came forward from who knows where—initials detached from the context in which they had been spoken: "U," "C," "D." I went out onto Christchurch Place and asked someone where I might find the nearest A.T.M.

In the smoke shop past the corner.

I ran to the smoke shop past the corner. The A.T.M. was down. I kept going, along Lord Edward Street, toward Dublin Castle. In a stone wall I found an A.T.M. The wall was stuffed with euros. What seemed like blocks later, I reached the Dame Street Taxi Rank, near Trinity College. To a kindly, graying driver, I said, "U.C.D." And where would I be going at U.C.D.? he asked. It's a great sprawling place, more than three hundred acres, and lying several miles from the city center.

"I don't know. I missed a bus. I'm supposed to be at a lacrosse match. Can you help me?"

It was a long ride, but not nearly long enough for the conversation that developed. At the first stoplight, he said, "And what might lacrosse be?"

I said it was football, basketball, and ice hockey in an advanced state of evolution. It was played with a solid rubber ball weighing a third of a pound and carried in a small basket at the end of a stick. If you grasped it like a hockey stick (hands apart) or even like a baseball bat (hands together) and swung it with full leverage, you could throw a lacrosse ball more than a hundred miles an hour. You could kill somebody. So players wear genital cups, pads, helmets, face masks. The idea is to throw the ball past a keeper into a netted goal.

How does a match begin? Does it begin like football?

It's like nothing you ever saw.

The ball is set on the ground at the center of the field. Close over it, two men face each other. The referee says, "Down!," as if he were addressing mastiffs. They go into deep knee squats with their stick heads back to back, inches apart but not touching the ball. After the referee blows a whistle, the face-off men grunt against each other and attempt by various maneuvers to gain possession of the ball. The face-off in women's lacrosse is more scenic. There is nothing collisional about women's lacrosse— no contact. The ball, held at shoulder height between the two opposing sticks, is flung upward as if on the jet of a fountain. Players converge from all directions and someone gains possession. Tribal face-offs were once quite similar to women's face-offs today. To begin a lacrosse game, Iroquois teams of the eighteenth century formed facing parallel lines, and a beautiful maiden (according to Samuel Woodruff, of Windsor, Ontario, writing in 1797) put the ball down on the field. Players from each team went to the ball "and with united bats raised it from the ground to such an elevation as gave a chance for a fair stroke."

In an ice-hockey face-off, the referee throws the puck down between two players and they fight it out. When my father, who was born in 1895, played basketball in high school and college, the referees tossed the ball into the air between two players after every score, and also at the start of each period. Basketball's face-off is known as the tip-off, and now, in college play, you see it only as it starts a game or in overtime. In lacrosse there is no more important play. After a score, the scored-upon team is not simply awarded the ball. It has to fight for it in a face-off, and teams that are good at facing off can score multiple consecutive goals while the other team, again and again, fails to gain possession of the ball. Because lacrosse substitutions are unlimited, many face-off players have become so specialized that they are known as FOGOs: Face Off, Get Off, to be replaced by a midfielder more skillful at attacking or defending. In the words of the professional midfielder Matt Striebel, of the Chicago Machine, "The FOGO has become one of the most highly sought-after positions in lacrosse, the object of intense recruiting. It is the most important position on the field, besides goaltending. A great FOGO is like a great place-kicker."

A FOGO's repertory includes but is not limited to the basic clamp, the pinch clamp, the rake, the jam, the plunger. Some FOGOs hold their sticks with the motorcycle grip (both palms down), the better to roll the head and clamp the ball. Danny Brennan, of Syracuse's 2008 N.C.A.A. champions, has said that the pinch clamp was his best move: "I try and suck my stick down low and beat his clamp. I use it a lot." A great general athlete is not going to be intimidated by a FOGO. The midfielder

Kyle Harrison, of Johns Hopkins' 2005 national champions and now a professional with the Denver Outlaws, told *Inside Lacrosse* magazine, "FOGOS are almost always very quick to the ball. So instead of trying to beat him to the ball, I forget the ball and focus on crushing the head of his stick with the shaft of my stick between my hands. Notice how I've slammed the shaft of my stick into the top part of the scoop of his stick. If I hit my shaft into the right part of his head, he's got no chance of stopping his head from spinning in his hands. So once I've pushed his head away from the ball I can use the shaft of my stick to pop the ball behind me where I can cut him off and get to the GB first. Just remember when you do this move do it hard and fast and relentlessly. There's no room for nice guys on face-offs." A GB is a ground ball. In 1888, Princeton's face-off man was Edgar Allan Poe. His granduncle (ibid.) wrote "The Raven."

As in the sibling sports, once you have the ball the idea is to free up someone, or free up yourself, to shoot—by picking and rolling, by dodging half a dozen ways, and even by resurrecting basketball's old-time weave (Hopkins' spaghetti offense). A ball thrown with such power that it does not even begin to curve toward the ground is called—as in baseball—a frozen rope. The N.R.A. would call it a round. As it passes above one or the other of the goalie's shoulders, he might not notice it. The lacrosse goal is vastly smaller than a soccer goal, of course, but—like a basketball hoop—it is larger than it seems to be. The apparent degree of difficulty of a parabolic basketball shot is diminished by the knowledge that the diameter of the hoop is nearly twice the diameter of the ball, which, as it drops in and begins to swish, occupies scarcely twenty-seven per cent of the targeted area. The lacrosse goalie defends a square plane, six feet on a side, framed by metal pipes. The surface area occluded by a goalie's body and the head of his stick is twenty-five per cent of the goal plane, give or take some fat. That leaves seventy-five per cent of a goal open at all times. A shooter has twenty-seven square feet always open, if not always in the same place.

Shooters aim for the lower corners, the upper corners, and the "5 hole" (between the goalie's legs). Good scorers can catch and shoot in a single motion. Good feeders make that possible. If an attacking player with his back to the goal takes a high feed and in one continuing windmill motion brings the head of his stick down past his knees and fires a shot into the net behind him, he has done a Canadian egg roll. An elevator is a shot that starts low and ends high. A wormburner is a shot that is low all the way. A bounce shot can be hard to stop, especially if it has sidespin on it. The Princeton coaches complain that Princeton players resist learning to put sidespin on a shot. (There have been exceptional exceptions.) Sidearm, sidespinning shots bounce higher, even past a goalie's shoulder. When a shot misses the goal and goes all the way over the end line, the ball is given to the player—attacker or defender—who was nearest the ball as it went out of bounds. In Tierney's words, "It's the only game in which if you miss the goal you get the ball back."

Goalies bait shooters. Goalies stand way over against one pipe and wait for some sucker to shoot into all that empty space— which has just been filled by the anticipating goalie. A shot that is fired straight into the pocket of a goalie's stick is a gumball. It is also called popcorn. The shooter should stay after practice and practice shooting. Goalies are so quick that they can sometimes "stuff" a point-blank shooter. An unguarded shot from three feet out can be caught by a goalie. Most shots, of course, come from greater distances, and when the goalie has the ball in his stick his eyes go back immediately to the source of the shot, because the goalie's teammate who was guarding the shooter will have turned upfield and is the first choice to receive the outlet pass. The shot, the stop, the outlet pass—the complete reversal of direction—will have taken as much as two seconds.

Of course, I didn't blurt out all this right there in that Dublin taxi—only the essence of it, of ninety per cent of it, in response to the driver's questions, which came one upon another and suggested a lifetime of attention to sporting games no matter how outlandish they might be. After we had been through Ranelagh and were just passing Royal Hospital Donnybrook, he asked if I had ever played lacrosse myself.

Once, I told him, but only for a season, at Deerfield Academy, in Massachusetts—a postgraduate year between high school and college. I played basketball there, compensating with quickness for a grave lack of height, and after a close and raucous game one Saturday night a teacher came through the departing crowd, stopped me on my way to the locker room, and said his name was Mr. Haviland, and that he was the coach of Deerfield lacrosse. He said come spring he would like me to try out for his team.

I might have been less surprised if he had asked me for a tip on the third at Gulfstream Park. In any case, that dialogue at courtside with him seems impossible, but this was 1949, when, nationally, about one-hundredth of one per cent of the population of the United States had ever heard of lacrosse, and five-thousandths of one per cent had ever played it. There had been no lacrosse at my high school, or, as far as I knew, at any other public high school in New Jersey. Besides, I had been on the high-school tennis team. I told Mr. Haviland that I had fiddled around with lacrosse sticks maybe ten times ever while I was growing up in Princeton, but I didn't play lacrosse, did not know how to play lacrosse.

His response was that I had just been playing it, in a sense, and that I could learn fairly quickly to play in the midfield, where defense would be much the same, and I could also learn quickly to scoop up a loose ball, after which my job would be to carry it to the other end of the field and throw it to a teammate who knew what he was doing. He said he thought I could be a real hoover, a ground-ball machine, and he would teach me the Baltimore crab (a twisting scoop on the dead run, also known as the Indian pickup). He said if I didn't learn to cradle well (create centrifugal force to keep the ball in my stick) I could hold the stick straight out in front of me, pocket up, ball inside it, as I sprinted up the field (a move known as walking the dog). "All you need to be is inn-terr-esst-edd," he said. I would before long be aware that the word "interested," pronounced in four discrete syllables, was not only a criterion statement of what a player had to be but also the highest compliment Mr. Haviland had to give.

All through spring vacation, I threw lacrosse balls at anything that would send them bouncing back to me. Some things didn't. They broke. On the high-school level in New England at that time, there was so little lacrosse that we had on our ten-game schedule only four high-school teams, and one of them—Manhasset—was from Long Island. The three others were Mount Hermon, Andover, and Exeter. Lacrosse had been played at Andover and Exeter in the eighteen-eighties but was not really established at either school until the nineteen-thirties. Andover's first modern coach was renowned for dancing nude in his living room while accompanying himself on the violin. Deerfield 10, Andover 6.

Absent other secondary schools to schedule, we played the junior-varsity team of Rensselaer Polytechnic Institute, the freshman lacrosse teams of Yale, Harvard, Dartmouth, and Williams, and, at West Point, the U.S. Military Academy plebes. Everybody was interested, one syllable at a time, and we won all those games. We were undefeated. We beat the plebes, 10–9, on the Plain. We beat Manhasset, 17–3, a scant six months before the unstoppable Jimmy Brown—by longtime consensus the greatest lacrosse player in the modern game—entered Manhasset High School as a freshman. Phew!

Our sticks were fashioned like shepherds' crooks from steamed and bent hickory. For every team then playing the game, they were made almost exclusively by the Iroquois. Where sticks were available from sporting-goods companies, they had been bought wholesale, primarily from Onondagas and Mohawks, Iroquoian tribes. The Iroquois made tens of thousands of sticks a year, each stick requiring about a year to cure, steam, bend, and string. It was not a particularly expandable industry. On average, the lower trunk of one good hickory yielded eight sticks, and this tended not only to affect the oak-hickory ratios in climax forests of northeastern America but also to limit the growth of the game. Sticks were idiosyncratic, as different as thumbprints. It was said that certain high-level lacrosse teams had the best sticks because the coaches had curried favor with the Indians. The pocket was shaped from woven stiff rawhide and leather thongs. As a result, the ball was harder to handle than it is now and spent more time loose on the ground.

Ask a modern player what he has in his hands, and, typically, he might say, "Cyber head on a black Swizzle Scandium." Next player: "A Penitrator head on a Gait Anarchy shaft." Next: "An Evolution 2.0 on a Kryptolyte shaft." Shafts are made of patented aluminum alloys, of graphite, of vanadium, of zirconium, of weapons-grade titanium. The teardrop heads are plastic and are bilaterally symmetrical (forget the shepherd's crook). The heads fit snugly and are secured with a screw. The revolution from wood to plastic took place in the nineteen-seventies, in a factory in Boston and another in Baltimore owned by a lacrosse all-American who had carried a wooden stick. The event is sometimes called the plasticization of lacrosse. It changed the game to the same great extent that pole-vaulting was changed when fibreglass replaced bamboo. With the new stick, a lacrosse player could do a great many things more surely, rapidly, and precisely—shoot, pass, pick up a loose ball, cradle to protect it. The fastest of running games became even faster, and even prettier to watch.

The custom stringing of tennis racquets is abecedarian compared with the subtleties that have developed in the stringing of lacrosse sticks. Nobody over nine uses a factory pocket, or so it seems. Some players carry around with them as many as seven heads. They bake their heads and reshape them. They carry different heads for different weather, because moisture changes the webbing. The "traditional pocket" of woven thongs is still in use, but more than ninety per cent of players go for nylon mesh, woven in various geometries, for the most part in vertical or horizontal diamonds. The ball rides in a pocket of assorted legal depths, and when it is thrown it first moves over the mesh toward the top of the stick. In the high and widest part of the mesh—woven in and out, from side to side—are the shooting strings, almost all of them laces made for hockey skates. There the ball trips, backspins, and fires. Out she goes in three digits, if you've got the rhythm and the muscle to make that happen. Lacrosse shops are not unlike fly-fishing shops in the bewildering range of what they have to offer, and players carry the topic forward into preoccupation, cryptoscience, and voodoo. They boil their mesh. They use Jergens lotion on their mesh. They buy pocket pounders and pocket screws that shape the mesh and hold it in place, like blocking a hat. They tune their shooting strings according to the kinds of shots they anticipate making. They tighten a "shooter," loosen one, take one out, thread another in the shape of a U. They string and otherwise shape the pocket to control its softness and legal depth.

This craft is too advanced for most lacrosse players, who turn to "stick doctors" for assistance. Usually, there are one or two on any team—for example, Charlie Kolkin and Alex Capretta at Princeton. Others describe their work as having gemlike characteristics. The University of Virginia has had its lacrosse sticks strung in California, by, so to speak, a plastic surgeon. His name is Lyle Tomlinson and he wore the number 34 when he played the game long ago. His "Pocket 34" is world famous—well, lacrosse-world famous. If a pocket can be called a sack—a real bag—it is deep and soft and will release a ball with a lot of "whip." Ask a lacrosse player how much whip is in his stick and he'll say something like "seven on a scale of ten." The more whip, the faster the shot. The more whip, the more erratic a throw is likely to be. Among other things, whip tends to bend trajectories downward. Bill Tierney is wary of whip. "It can cause bad passes," he explains. "Most mistakes are bad passes—thrown too low, for example, because of the whip in the passer's pocket."

These are things that players have confided to the writers of *Inside Lacrosse*:

I keep my pocket high in the stick, right under my bottom shooting string. I like a lot of hold at the top so I can take a deep windup when I shoot.

If you're a middie who shoots hard off the dodge or a guy who does most of his damage on set shots, you might want to have a decent amount of whip in your stick. It helps lock the ball in place under the shooting strings so you can really reach back and sling it. . . . If you want a lot of whip, tighten the top shooting string.

My best chance at scoring is by having a huge whip. . . . My theory is that if I don't even know where my shot is going, how the heck is a goalie going to guess where it's going?

Off Stillorgan Road, we turned in at University College Dublin, and the driver got out at a security hut to ask where, if anywhere, at U.C.D. we might find a lacrosse match between England and a team from America. There was no immediate response. Then: "Lacrosse?"

"Lacrosse," the driver affirmed, in a yes-of-course tone, as if suggesting that Cuchulain himself had played the game.

Security made calls on a mobile phone. At length, he seemed vindicated. No one else at U.C.D. knew from lacrosse. The one possibility was a sports ground on the far side of the college, and, because a campus road was blocked, we would have to detour outside the college to find the sports ground—about two miles.

So we started off again, the taxi driver asking how an aboriginal game had acquired in the first place such an unfathomable name.

The etymology has a lot of whip. A player's stick is also called a crosse. It is said that when the black robes of the seventeenth century saw the sticks of the Iroquois they thought of ecclesiastical crosiers. In some parts of France, cricket has been called *la crosse*. A game more or less like field hockey developed in France and was also called *le jeu de la crosse*. Prairie La Crosse, where the La Crosse River enters the Mississippi, is where the Winnebagos played, and where La Crosse, Wisconsin, is now.

Off Clonskeagh Road, we turned once again into the college, and a quarter mile later came upon a large parking area—buses, cars—and a fenced pitch covered with lacrosse players in red-and-white and orange-and-black. The driver said he would like to stay and watch.

In addition to the magazine *Inside Lacrosse*, the five books I am most indebted to in this piece of writing are "The Lacrosse Story," by Alexander M. Weyand and Milton R. Roberts (H. & A. Herman, Baltimore, 1965); "Lacrosse: A History of the Game," by Donald M. Fisher (The Johns Hopkins University Press, 2002), which began as a Ph.D. dissertation in history at the State University of New York at Buffalo; "Lacrosse: Technique and Tradition," by Bob Scott (The Johns Hopkins University Press, 1976, 2006), updated by David G. Pietramala and Neil A. Grauer; "American Indian Lacrosse: Little Brother of War," by Thomas

Vennum, Jr. (Smithsonian Institution Press, 1994); and "The Lacrosse History of the Boys' Latin School," by Mac Kennedy (unpublished).

The rules of lacrosse, learned or adapted primarily from Mohawks, were first set down, in pamphlet form, by George Beers, who later founded the *Canadian Journal of Dental Science*. The first game played by Beers' rules (and by players whose ancestors had lived in Europe) took place in 1867, Upper Canada College versus the Toronto Lacrosse Club—two years before the first game of American intercollegiate football (Rutgers 6, Princeton 4). On July 1, 1867, the British Parliament confederated Quebec, Ontario, New Brunswick, and Nova Scotia as the Dominion of Canada. Also on July 1, 1867—the date since celebrated as the birthday of the nation—the newly created Canadian Parliament passed an act confirming lacrosse as Canada's national game. In June, 1867, there were six lacrosse clubs in Canada. In December, there were eighty.

The first known news account describing lacrosse had appeared in Montreal in 1834, after Mohawks of the Caughnawaga Reserve (on the right bank of the St. Lawrence) demonstrated the game for white spectators. Senecas in Ontario played the game as well. Donald Fisher points out that Mohawks, Senecas, and the rest of the Six Nations of the Iroquois were on the wrong side in the American Revolution, and as a result a great many of them were driven into Canada. Generalizing on a grand scale, he says that Canadian whites thought of Indians "as their civilizational forebears," whereas "white Americans understood the natives within the context of a mythological western frontier, usually as savages hindering Manifest Destiny." In other words, John Quincy Adams did not play lacrosse. Meanwhile, white Canadians watched the Iroquois and began to try the game themselves.

On August 29, 1844, in the infield of Montreal's St. Pierre racecourse, seven white men faced five Indians in the first recorded interracial lacrosse game, in which the whites, according to the Montreal *Courier*, "were not a match for the red antagonists." In 1851, white lacrosse players won a game for the first time. On August 27, 1860, a game was played in Montreal before the Prince of Wales, the future Edward VII—whites versus Mohawks led by Sawatis Aientonni Baptiste Canadien, the Jimmy Brown of his time. In the goal for the Montreal Lacrosse Club was seventeen-year-old George Beers, who had been playing lacrosse since he was six. The game ended prematurely and inconclusively as a result of a "disputed Indian goal."

Fisher does not seem to care much for Beers, an antipathy that may relate to the following sample of the dentist's lacrosse philosophy. Beers: "The present game, improved and reduced to rule by the whites, employs the greatest combination of physical and mental activity white men can sustain in recreation and is as much superior to the original as civilization is to barbarism, base ball to its old English parent of rounders, or a pretty Canadian girl to any uncultivated squaw."

On September 25, 1867, the Toronto Lacrosse Club took on a team jointly representing Mohawks, Senecas, Cayugas, Oneidas, Onondagas, and Tuscaroras at the Toronto Cricket Club. Four thousand people watched the Six Nations win 3–2. On September 26, 1867, in Kingston, Ontario, delegates from twenty-nine lacrosse clubs established the Canadian National Lacrosse Association—George Beers, Secretary. Within a decade, Indians were banned from the association.

Their principal offense was that they earned money giving lacrosse exhibitions. They went to Saratoga and Troy in 1867, and to New York City in 1869. (Vennum: "The first white team in the United States, founded in December 1867 in Troy, New York, called itself the Mohawk Lacrosse Club.") The Indians put on lacrosse shows in the way that Buffalo Bill, sixteen years later, would put on Indian shows. Like modern lacrosse players, they spotted their faces with black patches. Buffalo Bill's Wild West may have helped kill off the lacrosse shows. Indians without cowboys were not as large a draw.

In 1869, though, Buffalo Bill was not even funct. At Jones Wood, a Manhattan park on the East River above Sixtieth Street, the Iroquois played the Blackfeet. The teams were invited by Thomas Van Cott. The gentrification of lacrosse was under way. They also played in Brooklyn and Jersey City. To challenge them, Canadians working in New York formed the Knickerbocker Lacrosse Club. The Knicks lost. Three years later, the New York club played the Montreal Lacrosse Club in Montreal. In those early days, lacrosse games were not played against the clock. They were won by the first team to score three goals. In the opinion of the Brooklyn *Daily Eagle*, lacrosse in the United States would prosper if the Americans won that game in Montreal, and die if they did not. It took Montreal fifteen and a half minutes to beat the Knickerbockers 3–0.

In the spring of 1876, Canadian players, both Indian and white, went to London, Belfast, Dublin, Glasgow, Edinburgh, Newcastle, Sheffield, Birmingham, Bristol, and—with the large effect still evident today—to Manchester. On Monday, June 26, 1876, at Windsor Castle, after tea, thirteen Indians defeated fourteen whites. One of the Indians placed a tomahawk at the feet of

Queen Victoria and then delivered an address in Mohawk. It wasn't short. Victoria wrote in her diary that lacrosse was "very pretty to watch." That Monday, June 26, was the day after the Lakota annihilated the Seventh Cavalry in the Battle of the Little Bighorn.

In 1877, New York University fielded the first U.S. college lacrosse team. Manhattan College rose to the challenge and played N.Y.U. in Central Park. Game called on account of darkness. A lacrosse exhibition involving club, college, and Indian teams was held at Gilmore's Garden, Twenty-sixth Street and Madison Avenue, in 1878. A year later, Gilmore's was renamed Madison Square Garden. In 1881, Harvard beat Princeton 3–0 for the first intercollegiate championship, the Chicago Lacrosse Club beat the Calumet Lacrosse Club for the Chicago championship, and on the Fourth of July the Union Lacrosse Club of Boston beat the Caughnawaga Mohawks before twenty thousand spectators on Boston Common.

In the three-goal era, Canadian Indians on their road trips into the United States sometimes scored three goals in the bat of an eye, mindful of their need to catch trains. In 1884, in Manhattan, Mohawks in an exhibition match with whites found themselves behind and in danger of losing. The New York *Times*: "They brought out all their clever tricks of dodging, passing, bumping, and knocking." In other words, they started playing flat-out lacrosse. The *Times* was getting inn-terr-esst-edd. It covered lacrosse in Montreal; for example, Montreal Shamrocks versus Caughnawaga Mohawks, September 6, 1886. Here is the *Times* describing the Shamrocks: "They opened the heads of Fenimore Cooper's gentle friends and jumped on their backs and body-checked them against trees and blackened their eyes and made their noses bleed." The Shamrocks were Irish Catholics who represented, according to Donald Fisher, the spread of Canadian lacrosse to the working class.

In 1909, when Hopkins was national champion, the runners-up were Harvard and, surprisingly, Columbia, which has no modern men's lacrosse team. If lacrosse could spread to Columbia, it could spread to British Columbia. Fisher: "During a June 1911 contest between the Vancouver L.C. and the New Westminster Salmonbellies, a crowd of ten thousand fans watched each team accumulate seventy-seven minutes in penalties." A Salmonbelly broke "an opponent's stick across his knee." The financier Bernard Baruch—adviser to Woodrow Wilson, adviser to Franklin Roosevelt—played lacrosse for what is now the City University of New York. Leon Miller, who coached there for twenty-eight years, was also a financier and a government adviser (and a professor and an engineer and a member of the American Stock Exchange). He is the only Cherokee in the National Lacrosse Hall of Fame.

The term "Gilman clear" was once understood only in Baltimore and is now understood as far from Baltimore as Ann Arbor, Fort Collins, and Los Angeles, not to mention Osaka. The Gilman School, K through 12, was founded on the campus of the Johns Hopkins University and was named for Hopkins' first president. If you look up Gilman's home page and click on "History," you will find eight short paragraphs relating to everything of great importance that has happened at Gilman since the late nineteenth century. Paragraph 3: "1947. Gilman wins its first Maryland Scholastic Association Lacrosse title. In the championship game against Boys Latin, trailing by four with five minutes left, senior mid-fielder Redmond C. S. 'Reddy' Finney wins five consecutive face-offs, leading to five unanswered goals and a Gilman victory. In 1968 he is named Gilman Headmaster, a decision that is based on formidable credentials not limited to these late-game heroics."

Six thousand spectators watched that high-school game, in a time when vaguely six thousand people had ever heard of lacrosse much west of Bethesda. The Gilman clear is like an NFL bomb with Hail Mary undertones—a pass thrown by a goalie from one end of the field to the other, sometimes with a recipient in mind. It was first executed by Cyrus Horine, who, as it happened, was Gilman's goalie in that championship game, in which he threw a Gilman clear in the final seconds after he "repulsed a last-minute Boys' Latin rally." The quotation is from "The Lacrosse History of the Boys' Latin School," whose eighty-three-thousand words, even without being read, say a great deal about lacrosse in Baltimore, where most of the boys on that field had been playing lacrosse since they were eight years old, or younger.

They were lax rats before the term was coined. A lax rat, as defined by "The Lacrosse Dictionary" (Glen Echo, Maryland), is "a kid that is never seen without a stick in his/her hand." In the words of David Marcus, a Boys' Latin alumnus, "In Baltimore, you see little children toting lacrosse sticks to an extent not seen elsewhere. They are told to throw against a brick wall, told always to use both hands, and told that this is an important part of your development. Never a mention to go home and improve your soccer skills. Always to improve lacrosse skills." For the better part of a century on the streets of Baltimore, kids carrying lacrosse sticks have played catch between one sidewalk and the other, denting cars. Lacrosse balls coming over playground fences also dented cars. In one asphalt playground in winter, Claxton J. "Okey" O'Connor, a teacher at Boys' Latin, on Brevard Street, taught third and fourth graders Circle Lacrosse. In the center of a circle about twenty feet in diameter was a five-foot steel pole set in a can filled with concrete. At the top of the pole was a netted basketball hoop, attached vertically. Teams shot lacrosse balls at the hoop. No one could go into the circle, or "crease." Grade-school kids in Baltimore took lacrosse sticks to class (and still do), in order to get in a little stickwork during recess. With overlapping rec lacrosse, indoor rec lacrosse, travel-team lacrosse, and school lacrosse, a player growing up in Baltimore today plays nine months a year. Franklin Knipp, who grew up in Baltimore and played lacrosse at St. Paul's School there in the nineteen-forties, remembers his math teacher Howdy Myers telling students to take lacrosse sticks on dates. They did what they were told. Mr. Myers was also the lacrosse coach.

In the Baltimore *Sun*, high-school lacrosse had long since become front-page-sports news, a fact attributed by Joe Finn, the archivist at the National Lacrosse Museum and Hall of Fame, to the charming "insularity" of—as Baltimore is called—Charm City. Finn: "It never occurred to Baltimoreans that lacrosse wasn't played anywhere else." Two public high schools—Baltimore City College and Baltimore Polytechnic Institute, insularly known as City and Poly—had been lacrosse powers since, respectively, 1902 and 1912. The private schools (and other public high schools) took it up in the twenties and thirties—so many of them that the schools of Baltimore had to be assigned to divisions like modern professional sports teams, those with the better records playing it off at the end of the season. In 1926, Rosabelle Sinclair, a teacher at Baltimore's Bryn Mawr School, introduced lacrosse to girls in America. She had recently arrived from Scotland, where women's lacrosse began. In 1931, the students at Boys' Latin voted to drop baseball for lacrosse, as two other private schools had done earlier. Even in the nineteen-forties and fifties, Baltimore high-school lacrosse could draw upward of five thousand people, and was becoming, if anything, increasingly intense. In 1962, after a brawl erupted that seemed to be going light-years out of control, a Boys' Latin midfielder seized a timer's pistol, aimed it at the brawl, and fired. Exeunt brawl.

Baseball has revived to some extent in Baltimore schools, and there are play-offs in baseball, too. David Marcus once remarked to me that twenty-five spectators might show up for the baseball, while eight thousand will turn out for the finals of high-school lacrosse. "There is an element of theatre at high-school lacrosse games, people standing in the same places, alumni for decades—a lot of people. You see the whole community."

"Do you ever go to a high-school football game?" I asked him.

He said, "There is no reason you would do that to yourself."

In summer in the eighteen-seventies in Newport, Rhode Island, there was an annual array of sporting events that might now be called the Lockjaw Games. Foxhunting, lawn tennis, horse racing, yachting, and polo were the staples, but there were track-and-field events and, as a sort of sideshow, lacrosse, with Iroquois

teams on exhibition as well as other Canadian and United States
clubs. James Gordon Bennett, Jr., was there—publisher of the
New York *Herald*, president of the Westchester Polo Club. His
newspaper reported that lacrosse was "the talk of Newport,"
adding, "the universal verdict is that lacrosse is the most remarkable, versatile, and exciting of all games of ball." Fisher's "History"
reminds us that Bennett "advocated the extermination of native
peoples." When the Caughnawaga Mohawks played an intrasquad
game in Newport, August Belmont refereed.

In 1878, track-and-field athletes from Baltimore watched
lacrosse at the Lockjaw Games. From the Iroquois there, they
bought balls and sticks. They took them home, and in Mount
Washington, in the northern part of the city, played the first-ever
game of lacrosse in Baltimore. A thousand people came out to see
it. Four thousand watched a lacrosse exhibition in old Newington
Park a few months later. Also in 1878, lacrosse took place but not
root in Detroit, Buffalo, and San Francisco. No Eastern tribe, as far
as research has yet shown, ever played lacrosse anywhere near the
Chesapeake Bay. In ice ages, when a continental ice sheet forms, it
begins not at the North Pole (to go sliding down over the globe)
but at a specific spreading center perhaps thousands of miles south,
from which the developing ice spreads out to the west, south, east,
and north. For example, the spreading center of the most recent
ice sheet in North America was in the Otish Mountains, in Quebec. Baltimore is the spreading center of modern lacrosse. Why
Baltimore? You would need a doctorate in urban psychology to
begin to guess at an answer, but meanwhile you have Joe Finn and
his "insular city": "Most Baltimoreans think if you went outside
the city limits you went off the edge of the world. If something
got into Baltimore, it tended to stay and develop." The game was

fostered by the argentocracy of Baltimore. Players who practiced in Druid Hill Park and formed in 1883 the Druid Lacrosse Club were "sons of wealthy merchants," as one of their coaches told the Montreal *Evening Post*. Note the interest of a Canadian newspaper in the birth of lacrosse in Baltimore.

The Johns Hopkins University, twelve years old, entered the competition in 1888, and became the spreading center within the spreading center. The Hop, as lacrosse players call it, was the farmer of Baltimore high-school lacrosse. Hopkins players went to City College and gave talks. They helped the students obtain sticks. They taught them the game in Druid Hill Park. In 1902, Hopkins players got things started at City, and by 1912, City and Poly were both playing formal schedules. Lacrosse in those earliest years became the number-one sport at the university, its teams fed by City and Poly. Not many years later, the Hop fostered lacrosse in Baltimore's private schools, and Hopkins lacrosse teams drew heavily from them, too. In this manner, Hopkins was on its way to (at this writing) forty-four national championships, under storied coaches like Bill Schmeisser, Howdy Myers, Bob Scott, Henry Ciccarone, and Dave Pietramala. Howdy Myers, earlier, was the schoolteacher who told his students to take lacrosse sticks on dates. Schmeisser was known as the father of lacrosse, an honor he has shared with others. Lacrosse has more fathers than the Society of Jesus.

In 1940, the Baltimore *Sun* declared, "It is time now . . . to put lacrosse among the distinctly Maryland things of wide reputation along, say, with the literary works of Poe and Mencken, certain superior cookery styles, and liberal tolerance," a sentiment that went untoppled for twenty-six years, until Spiro Agnew was elected Governor. After voices in the academic wilderness were heard asserting that the role of money in athletics in higher education "contradicted the intellectual mission of the American university," Hopkins further bleached its football and basketball programs and further elevated lacrosse. A Howdy Myers recruiting class at Hopkins would typically include all but one or two of the high-school lacrosse players who were named first-team All-Maryland.

After we played the plebes at Army, in 1949, we did not get into our bus and depart immediately for Massachusetts. We stayed at West Point long enough to watch the Army varsity play the Hop. Army lacrosse in those years was known—as were other college teams—for encouraging football players to come out for lacrosse and contribute to the physical possibilities of the game. Army had outstanding football teams in the nineteen-forties, and those big tackles, guards, and fullbacks looked intimidating even in lacrosse shorts. There was an ambulance beside the field. The Hopkins players looked sort of thin and pale, as if they had been up all night studying organic chemistry. They looked anemic beside the military cadets. The first casualty occurred not long after the opening face-off. Others followed throughout the game. The ambulance had a busy day. The cadets just crushed those little pre-meds, or whatever else they might have been. Yet, time and time again, as a Hopkins player was creamed by a cadet and was falling wounded toward the ground, he would flick the ball into the Army goal. Army 6, Hopkins 10. Hopkins finished the season with the national championship, its third in three years.

Baltimore's high-school lacrosse was on its way to becoming a game not of the whole city but of specific neighborhoods, like

Mount Washington and Roland Park, well north of the city's center. In the sixties, Bill Tanton wrote in the Baltimore *Evening Sun*: "A Roland Park woman will drive her Mercedes-Benz out Falls Road to St. Paul's School, where she will stand atop the hill overlooking the lacrosse field and watch her son play. At one point in the action, she is guaranteed to shriek, in very un-Roland-Park-like tones, 'Ride him, Skippy, ride him!' (When it comes to athletes with names like Skippy or Booty or Buzzy or even Myrt, lacrosse people are in a class by themselves.)"

Their names can indeed tend to suggest inverted echoes of privilege. Cookie. Chooch. In 1929, J. Cavendish "Cabbage" Darrell scored seven goals for Boys' Latin against Forest Park. And eight decades later we have Ashton Hotchkiss and Brogan Van-Skoik, never mind that the teams they have played for are, respectively, Roanoke and Potsdam. I once asked a basketball coach to go to a lacrosse game with me, and he said, "I'm not going to watch a game played by the sons of doctors and lawyers." It was his conviction that if a family had a garage, let alone a car, no one who grew up in that house could possibly be tough enough to drive the middle. Historian Fisher does not seem to be disagreeing when he says, "Lacrosse allowed sportsmen to engage in a spirited and manly activity removed from the realm of their socio-economic inferiors." Even a college lacrosse coach—more than half a century ago—remarked of lacrosse that it was "strictly a button-down sport." In the nineteen-eighties, a coach at a schoolboy lacrosse camp said to the writer Ramsey Flynn, of *Baltimore Magazine*, "You're not going to find too many people out here in *bowling* shirts. You know what I mean?"

David Marcus, musing on "the psychological hold on the community" that characterized lacrosse in large parts of his home town, has remarked, "I think that's one of the things that makes lacrosse really strange. I wouldn't normally associate wealthy Americans with obsession over a sport."

After Bear Stearns collapsed, its lacrosse team was absorbed by Bank of America. And the Merrill Lynch Bulls faded into history. But the teams of Credit Suisse, Citigroup, Barclays Capital, and Morgan Stanley survived after a fashion in a league called Gotham Lacrosse. Financial firms and other companies have long been top-heavy with lacrosse players, not only in New York but also in the investment colonies—needless to say, in Baltimore. In the way that if you were a colonel in the Swiss Army you were also president of the Schweizerischer Bankverein or the Schweizerische Kreditanstalt, if you were the C.E.O. of a Baltimore corporation you were probably born with a silver stick in your mouth.

As the game has spread, though, it has, in Bill Tanton's words, "been losing its buttons," in Baltimore as elsewhere. Ramsey Flynn, writing in *Baltimore Magazine* in the nineteen-eighties, said: "Most of the local lacrosse leaders have wanted it to grow. A minority had wanted it to grow 'only among the right people.' There was a power struggle in recent years, and the socialists won." Fisher: "The notion of lacrosse as an exclusive game for gentlemen and ladies . . . found only on the playing fields of elite universities and preparatory schools was dead."

Dying maybe, but not dead. In Dublin, watching televised soccer over stout, Princeton's team physician, Margot Putukian, asked Bill Tierney if, among his players, "anybody at all comes from a working-class background." The coach thought a while, and mentioned the son of an English teacher and the son of another college lacrosse coach, but then he fell out of touch with the faintest intimation of peasantry, and—returning to her question—said, "Nobody."

While I was in the taxi trying to catch up with the team that morning, the driver asked me to what extent black athletes play the game I was describing. Not to a great enough extent, I said, as—I'm not making this up—we raced down Donnybrook Road. The recent spread of lacrosse has been a geographic, not a demographic, phenomenon. In the United States population, the percentage of African Americans is about thirteen and the percentage of black lacrosse players is at best about 1.3. I said something to the effect that while there have been some remarkable exceptions, nearly all lacrosse players are white, and more blacks would surely escalate, in a number of ways, an already mercurial game. The Irish taxi driver said, "Yes, they have pace, more pace."

I thought of some of the black exceptions. For example, the All-American Kyle Harrison (Hopkins '05). The All-American Damien Davis (Princeton '03). The fathers of Davis and Harrison are medical doctors. Kurt Schmoke (Yale '71) played high-school lacrosse at Baltimore City College, spent two years at Oxford as a Rhodes Scholar, became mayor of Baltimore, and is now Dean of the Howard University School of Law. Morgan State University, traditionally black, started a lacrosse program in 1969. Six years later, they were beating undefeated Washington and Lee. The two most heavily recruited high-school seniors in 2007 were Rhamel and Shamel Bratton, identical twins, who played for Huntington High School on Long Island and went on to the Final Four as freshman midfielders at Virginia. Blog: "These guys are lightning rods. They play with flash and flair and attitude, possessing the potential at all times to light up any defender." Jim Thorpe wasn't white, either. The A.P.'s "greatest athlete of the first half of the

twentieth century" was a Sac and Fox Indian who learned lacrosse not in his childhood years in Oklahoma but in a school in
Pennsylvania established by the U.S. government to strip Indians of
their heritage and render them culturally white. Red Cloud sent
his grandson there; Spotted Tail, five of his children. With Thorpe
playing, the Carlisle Indians beat Navy. They beat Hopkins.

In the 2001 N.C.A.A. championship game, Mikey Powell
of Syracuse (short, white, and sensational) was a freshman. His
two older brothers had both been stars of Syracuse lacrosse. The
Princeton goalie was Trevor Tierney, Coach Tierney's son—a
Shakespearean situation if lacrosse could ever produce one. The
defenseman who covered Mikey Powell was Damien Davis. Blog:
"Mikey is one of the most awesome and totally tubular cool
players in collegiate lacrosse history. A four-time first-team All-
American, he became the first (and only) player to win the Jack
Turnbull Award as the top attackman in Division I lacrosse four
consecutive times." Princeton was ahead 9 to 8 with sixteen seconds to go. Syracuse had the ball, and Coach John Desko called a
time-out to decide what to do, what to try, what play to run.
Mikey Powell, describing that moment to *Inside Lacrosse*: "I will
never forget approaching the huddle. Everyone was silent, including Desko. He just stared at me for the first 30 seconds of our
timeout as if he were looking beyond my eyes into my heart to
see if I really 'wanted' the ball. My natural reaction was to stare
back into his eyes and after a while I gave him a nod to let him
know I was ready. He didn't pull out the chalkboard; all he said
was, 'We are giving the ball to 22; get us to overtime.' I wasn't the
best player on my team. I was young and inexperienced. I was
matched up against Damien Davis, one of the best defensemen in
the country. Forty thousand people were on their feet. The game

was on ESPN. My brothers were on the field. I was five inches shorter and 50 pounds lighter than my defenseman. But these were all afterthoughts. . . . All I was thinking was, 'I'm going to split Damien and throw a behind-the-back pass to Mike Springer on the doorstep once Ryan Mollett slides.' Well, Coach Bill Tierney must have told the D not to slide, and I was able to get in front of the cage and go five-hole on Trevor Tierney. The number one trait that I feel clutch players need to possess is confidence. . . . I feel that on lacrosse's biggest stage weaker and less confident players' weaknesses become exposed and clutch players rise beyond their abilities to become almost superhuman in the spotlight. If you're reading this and wondering if you're a clutch player, you're not. A clutch player knows he is." Syracuse 9, Princeton 9. Overtime.

In the Princeton huddle before play resumed, Bill Tierney studied Damien Davis, looking beyond his eyes and into his neurocity to see if maybe Damien—once burned, twice vulnerable—would prefer that Ryan Mollett cover Powell. Tierney said, "Can you cover him?" Looking directly into Tierney's eyes, Davis fairly smoldered. He said, "I've got him." About three minutes into the overtime, Syracuse got control of the ball, and took a time-out. Again they gave the ball to Mikey Powell. As play resumed, Powell made a move on Davis. Davis hit him with a back-check and stripped him. Davis scooped the ball off the ground. Before long, it was in the Syracuse net, for Tierney's sixth national championship in ten seasons.

Jimmy Brown was born on St. Simons Island, off mainland Georgia. From the age of eight, he grew up on Long Island, where his mother worked as a domestic servant. At Syracuse University in the nineteen-fifties, he became, yes, the greatest football player in the school's history (on his way to becoming the greatest running back in the history of the National Football League), but he was not, in the usual manner, a football player who played lacrosse. He was a lacrosse player who played football. He loved lacrosse, called it his favorite sport. "Lacrosse is probably the best sport I ever played. . . . I could express myself fully in lacrosse. I could run two hundred yards at a stretch. I could duck between players. I could feel free to make the plays that suited me best. It wasn't like football or basketball, where coaches tell you what foot to put down." He had grown up in lacrosse—Manhasset High School '53. He was not a massive defenseman with a long stick killing intruders. He was a massive midfielder with a four-foot stick that looked a lot shorter in his hands. Cradling with one wrist, he would lower his left shoulder, and—in various versions—say, "Look out! I'm coming through." Bob Scott, head coach at Hopkins then and for twenty years, remembers Jimmy Brown as "a man playing with boys." Scott continues, "He weighed two-twenty-eight. Holy mackerel! The thighs were huge. I don't think anybody would try to take Jimmy Brown. Mount Washington guys threw body checks at him—at a brick wall. You couldn't double-team him. He'd just go through it. He just went by people and fired it in the goal. He startled the lacrosse world, he was so good."

In 1941, in Annapolis, Maryland, the lacrosse team of the United States Naval Academy refused to take the field if Lucien Alexis, Jr., of Harvard, did, too. Alexis was black. Harvard sent him home.

Since the National Lacrosse Hall of Fame was established, in 1957, about three hundred men have been elected to membership, a hundred and twenty of them from Baltimore, others from nearby. ("It never occurred to Baltimoreans that lacrosse wasn't played anywhere else.") Baltimoria is a name sometimes used for the game's local spread of activity and influence. The District of Columbia is in Baltimoria. Potomac, Bethesda, and Falls Church are in Baltimoria. Baltimoria begins at the Baltimore Beltway, reaches north (Mays Chapel, Timonium, Cockeysville), west (Catonsville, Ellicott City), over the bay to the Eastern Shore (Chestertown, etc.), and south in Anne Arundel County down a lacrosse archipelago through Glen Burnie, Severn, and Severna Park to Annapolis. Look through a Division I team roster and you will see those hometown names. Ravi K. Sitlani—coach, manager, and full-time head of English lacrosse—is still a little awestruck by the impression he formed, years ago, on his first visit to Annapolis: "That did it—lacrosse goals in people's gardens."

In 2008, the N.C.A.A. lacrosse Final Four occurred in the stadium of football's New England Patriots, in Foxboro, Massachusetts. This was a breakout move. The national lacrosse championships have traditionally been held in Baltimoria, with very few exceptions, not among them Philadelphia, which is in Baltimoria. The Foxboro final drew forty-nine thousand spectators. The 2009 Final Four was in Foxboro also; and the source of this phenomenon was Bill Belichick, coach of the Patriots. Belichick has been seen on the sidelines at lacrosse games at the Hop. He has warmed up Hopkins goalies. Bill Tierney's winter days in his office have included calls from Belichick. The Jimmy Brown of football coaches, Belichick loves lacrosse. When Navy made it to the N.C.A.A. final a few years ago, Navy's coach told his players, just before they took the field, that someone wanted to address them. The midshipmen did not at first recognize him, but—as their coach told the writer Mike Keegan—a short way into the talk one player's face said it all: "Holy shit! That's Bill Belichick!"

Belichick grew up in Annapolis, played lacrosse at Annapolis High School, played lacrosse in a postgraduate year at Andover, and was captain of lacrosse at Wesleyan University. Belichick's three children played lacrosse, and still—from stick to stick—fling the ball around with their father. In importance among all sports at Annapolis High School, lacrosse was number one. Belichick's own father was a football coach at the Naval Academy, where two guys from the Hop had colonized lacrosse sixty years before. While Belichick was in grade school, middle school, and high school, the Navy midshipmen were the national lacrosse champions in eight consecutive seasons.

In the early twentieth century, a New York City public-schools championship lacrosse trophy featured an Indian sitting on a rock with a lacrosse stick in his hand above a base covered with arrowheads and scalps. The several thousand Canadians who were living in the city in the eighteen-seventies and onward had not been alone in planting lacrosse and creating the historic Brooklyn and Manhattan clubs. In 1879, when the United States National Amateur Lacrosse Association was founded in New York, its first president was Hermann Oelrichs, a wealthy shipper who had come to New York from—where else?—Baltimore. Such colonists and collectibles notwithstanding, lacrosse atrophied over time in New York City proper, and the fact that Long Island became the second great hotbed of American lacrosse owes itself in large degree to still another Baltimore colonial. This was Howdy Myers, who took over as coach at Hofstra in 1950—the same Myers who had told his players at St. Paul's School in Baltimore to carry their lacrosse sticks when courting girls, the same

Myers who had left St. Paul's to coach Johns Hopkins for three years, in each of which his teams were national collegiate champions (the Hopkins team that I saw being maimed as they defeated Army was coached by Howdy Myers).

To Hempstead and Hofstra, he took the Hopkins system of growing your own players from the crib locally. Myers was not the inventor of Long Island lacrosse but he surely amplified it. For five years or so, it had been played in the high schools of Sewanhaka, Garden City, and Manhasset, and almost nowhere else. Hempstead, Levittown—all over Nassau County—Myers tirelessly went to school after school, talking lacrosse, and setting up intramural programs that before long would bloom as varsity teams. This led to weekend clinics for first graders and travelling teams whose players were eight years old. Four thousand people will show up today to see Garden City take on Manhasset. Long Island has essentially become equivalent to Baltimore as a nursery of the game's primary stars.

In the way that a placer miner can look at a nugget and say what stream it came from, a lacrosse coach can watch an unknown player for a while and write down his home address. Bill Tierney is nothing if not candid in delivering such descriptions: "Baltimore kids are slicker, more highly skilled, coached better at a younger age. Long Island youth coaching is not as skillful—and the guys play like football players." Tierney is from Long Island. His close friend Bob Scott, twenty-year head coach at Hopkins, said to me about Long Islanders: "They're tougher. They're all public-schoolers." The writer Mike Keegan: "You'd take the hard-nosed middie over the finesse attackman any day. . . . Public-school lax is where it's at." Some bloggers may be coaches, to wit: "Baltimore: Always have good sticks and tend to play more of a finesse game. Because most of them tend to be prep school kids, they shy away from physicality, and bring amazing stick skills to the table. Baltimore tends to produce the best individual players. Long Island: They tend to play like they were raised: tough. Count on them playing nasty, and not caring if you don't like it. Long Island produces the best team players."

"Different pockets, different styles," Tierney says, adding that the fingerprints are also different "between public schools on Long Island and public schools in upstate New York." Upstate New York is a term narrowed in lacrosse to mean anything within seventy miles of Syracuse, which is the game's third major hotbed. Syracuse is no Baltimore colony. It is more like America before contact. The Iroquois are there. An Onondaga reservation full of lacrosse goals is eight miles south of town. Lacrosse players from the Six Nations have played on national-championship Syracuse teams, of which there have been a great many. Over the years, the effect of the Native Americans may have been less tangible than inspirational, but north-central New York is where they are, and north-central New York is where the high schools are that provide half of Syracuse's lacrosse players. On the reservations, as in Canada, not far away, lacrosse has long been played indoors—mainly in hockey rinks, with goals less than half the size of outdoor goals, and goalies so thickly padded they look like parade floats. In the words of the pro Matt Striebel, "Canadians are terrific finishers. Shooting at four-by-four goals with a goalie dressed like the Michelin man, they develop stick skills that exceed the outdoor game." This tribal and Canadian influence is perennially strong in the rosters of Syracuse. In ones and twos, maybe, Syracuse will recruit players from places like Connecticut and California. Nobody from Baltimore is on the Syracuse team.

Like Long Island, Syracuse plays tough. Like Baltimoria, they play with finesse. They have also somehow accelerated an already fast game. At a coaches' convention some years ago, Roy Simmons, Jr., whose father preceded him as coach of Syracuse, was asked to close the proceedings by revealing some of the inner mysteries of Syracuse lacrosse. Simmons got up, faced the audience, and gave a six-word speech. He said, "We dare our players to dream." Then he pressed a button and a screen lighted up with a blistering montage of fast fast-breaks, each one resulting in a Syracuse goal.

In 2009, after Syracuse and Cornell went into overtime in the national-championship game, Cornell won the face-off, and soon Ryan Hurley, a Cornell star, cradling on his right, went into a dodge and threatened Syracuse with sudden death. Sid Smith, a Syracuse defenseman, stripped Hurley with a perfectly timed slap check, and picked up the ball, reversing the direction of play. The clear that Smith began delivered the ball to Cody Jamieson, of the Syracuse attack, who fired a shot with such assurance that he did not watch it go into the net. Instead, he turned instantly, sprinted the length of the field, and jumped into an embrace with Sid Smith. Jamieson and Smith, Iroquois, are from Six Nations of the Grand River, Ontario.

Norio Endo, who graduated from Hopkins in 1956, started lacrosse in Japan. He arranged for Coach Bob Scott to go to Japan and give clinics. The whole Hopkins team has been to Japan twice. Meanwhile, in the geography of lacrosse, Los Angeles was at least as eccentric as Tokyo when Mike Allan, who grew up in Baltimore, began a coaching career that has included club teams at U.C.L.A. and U.C. Santa Barbara and the Los Angeles Riptide, a professional team that failed to survive the economic decompression of 2008. In 2004, Scott Hochstadt, who grew up in Baltimore, founded the Starz Lacrosse Club for high-school-age players in Los Angeles, and in 2007 founded City Starz, introducing lacrosse to the inner-city neighborhoods of South Central Los Angeles. Bill Tierney: "A family moves from Baltimore and into a new town somewhere, and starts a kids program and a youth program, and once it takes off it's like a brush fire. Minnesota, California, Utah, Colorado—what we talk about is connecting the dots." Or the fires. In a big way, Tierney himself was to become such a connection. Soon after the 2009 season, his twenty-second at Princeton, he announced that he was moving west to coach the University of Denver's men's lacrosse team, in part, he said, to help augment the nationwide expansion of Division I lacrosse, and in part to join his son Trevor, a 2001 All-American and former professional with the Denver Outlaws, who would become his father's assistant coach.

The Big Bang that has occurred in lacrosse does not exclude the eccentricities in the game's geographic history, but the great expansion originated mainly in Baltimore and Strong Island, as Nassau and Suffolk counties are known in the game; and so many colonies have developed nationwide that the "hotbed era" is said to be over. When people not long ago used terms like All-America or mentioned what they thought was the best lacrosse team in the country, "the country," in Bob Scott's words, "was a small world of Eastern collegiate lacrosse, even high-school lacrosse," but, as the colonies grew, Little League lacrosse and rec lacrosse became ever-larger factors in shortening the distances between the dots. By the late nineteen-eighties, Steve Stenersen, a director of the Lacrosse Foundation, was saying (somewhat incompletely), "Lacrosse is no longer a sport played only by Indians and preppies."

In Ohio in 1941, Oberlin played Kenyon in the first inter-collegiate lacrosse game west of the Appalachians. Now Brig-ham Young University flies east over both the Rockies and the Appalachians to play Florida State in Tallahassee. In the late nineties, a Princeton defenseman from Denver East, a public high school, played on three consecutive national-championship teams and was named All-American. Following Army's and Navy's long traditions in lacrosse, the Air Force Academy took the game into Colorado in the nineteen-sixties, as did a small group of Eastern colonials in Denver, with the result that Colorado Springs, Den-ver, Boulder, and Fort Collins are outlying fragments of Baltimo-ria. The Vail Lacrosse Shootout, three thousand participants, is one of the game's more prominent tournaments. Dick's Sport-ing Goods Park, in Commerce City (Denver), has twenty-four lighted fields, one of them in a stadium that seats eighteen thou-sand people. Dick's Sporting Goods Park has started an annual one-day LaxFest involving three hundred teams, every known gender, and six thousand players. It gets dusty. In 2008, the Uni-versity of Denver travelled east and played Ohio State University in Ohio Stadium, Columbus, before 29,601 spectators, setting an attendance record for a regular-season lacrosse game. Truth be told, the lacrosse game was a prelim, and after it ended 45,700 additional fans came into the stadium for Ohio State's annual intrasquad spring-football game. Truth be also told, there are only two N.C.A.A. Division I lacrosse teams west of the Mississippi River: Denver and Air Force. But—hold on—the sixteen best college teams in the country are those that get into the N.C.A.A.-championship tournament, and Denver has been there.

There is a men's lacrosse team at the newly established Uni-versity of California, Merced. In Division I women's lacrosse,

Fresno State has joined the University of Oregon, Stanford, U.C. Berkeley, U.C. Davis, St. Mary's College (of Moraga, California), and Denver in the Mountain Pacific Sports Federation. Listed, in recent computer rankings, among the top thirty-five boys' lacrosse teams in the country are Saint Andrew's School, Boca Raton, Florida; Brother Rice High School, of Bloomfield Hills, Michigan; Highland Park Boys Lacrosse League, in Dallas County, Texas; Arapahoe High School, in Littleton, Colorado; Coronado High School, in Coronado, California; and Saint Ignatius College Preparatory, in San Francisco. Beverly Hills High School had an ambidextrous shooter who scored fifty-four goals in his sophomore year. Dougherty Valley High School, in San Ramon, California, fielded its first lacrosse team in 2008, as did Katy High School, Katy, Texas. Connecting the dots, there are lacrosse camps for boys or girls in Minnesota, Michigan, California, Florida, Oregon, Utah, Tennessee, South Carolina, Georgia, Texas, Arizona, Ohio, Alabama, and New Mexico, among other places.

Pre-contact, aboriginal, American Indian lacrosse was played, in its various forms, almost wholly to the east of the Mississippi River, but to some extent in Wisconsin and Minnesota, even in the Dakotas. Native American lacrosse was not played, in other words, in seventy-five per cent of what is now the United States. Not unmindful of the explosive growth of the modern game, the Six Nations of the Iroquois have undertaken an analogous expansion—a twenty-first-century attempt to foster the spread of Indian lacrosse! Reservation to reservation, they have gone west promoting the game, resuscitating Menominees in Wisconsin, waking up Ojibwes in Minnesota. As much as a decade ago, the Iroquois Nationals went to Denver and set up lacrosse clinics for Western and Southwestern tribes.

All ages, races, and genders, we now have something approaching five hundred thousand lacrosse players in the United States. There are more than three thousand boys' high-school teams and nearly twenty-four hundred girls' teams. In 1929, public and private, the number of high-school lacrosse teams was under twenty. It grew to about four hundred by 1976, and has gone exponential since then. One of the countless differences between, for example, 2007 and 2009 was six hundred new lacrosse teams. In the public high schools of New Jersey, lacrosse began in the nineteen-sixties. There are fifteen thousand high-school lacrosse players in New Jersey now, five thousand in Texas, five thousand in Minnesota, ten thousand in California.

Inevitably, eventually, some school teams would come back from distant places to bite the hand that fed them. In 2004, Torrey Pines High School, of San Diego, beat Garden City High School, in Garden City, Long Island. In 2003, Michigan's Brother Rice beat Landon, a Bethesda boys' school that is always one of the best in Baltimoria. In 2006, Cherry Creek (a Denver public high school) beat Wantagh High School, in Wantagh, Long Island, 6 to 3. Cherry Creek killed Strong Island, playing three games in three days against three different high schools and winning them all. In 2008, Cherry Creek went to Baltimore and upset the city's number-one-ranked Loyola Blakefield. Also in Baltimore, a unified team from Fort Collins high schools beat St. Paul's. Saint Andrew's went twenty-two-and-one and beat Lake Brantley for the state championship of Florida, where the game is played from Pensacola to Jacksonville and as far south as the Keys (the Key West Conchs). In the previous season, Saint Andrew's had beaten McDonogh, of Owings Mills, Maryland, a traditional power in secondary-school lacrosse; and in one of those twenty-two wins in 2008—chewing on the carpals, metacarpals, and phalanges of Baltimoria—the school from Florida beat Boys' Latin.

At numerous colleges and universities, club lacrosse is the only way the game is played. At schools like the University of Michigan, the club team is mocked as a "virtual varsity." There are club-lacrosse national championships. Michigan won in 2008 and 2009. In the 2007 final, Brigham Young clobbered Oregon at Pizza Hut Park, in Frisco, Texas. There are club-lacrosse national rankings, club-lacrosse All-America teams. In geography, college club-lacrosse is more widespread than its older brother, and in numbers is somewhat larger. Lacrosse seems to have an N.C.A.A. and a Virtual N.C.A.A.

If the game has been in recent times like a fast-rising river, Title IX stands in it like a dam. The river flows over it, surely, but it impounds a lot of water behind it. Under Title IX, the "equal opportunity" clause is difficult to meet in a sport whose men's-team rosters approach double the number of players on a women's team. A prodigious frequency of strategic substitution characterizes the men's but not the women's game; also, injuries sideline male players—sometimes a whole row of them at the end of the bench, in slings or with crutches—whereas women's rules forbid contact. If, overall, your athletic teams reflect the gender ratio in your school at large, you are O.K. with Title IX, but nobody has yet conceived an antidote to football, and that puts particular pressure on any other kind of men's team, especially a new one. The solution—drop football—is evidently too obvious. "Lacrosse is new, no other sport is new," Bill Tierney remarks. "Some have cut wrestling, baseball . . . but lacrosse is trying to add something." Meanwhile—K through 12—rec and Little League and school lacrosse are preparing a superfluity of male players whose windows of opportunity are all but shut in the N.C.A.A. They want to keep on playing, naturally, and the surest way is through an option that does not have to conform to Title IX. You pay three thousand dollars and join a club. In Tierney's words, "They're coming in a different doorway." In comes the Parade of the Virtual Varsities, led by Michigan, Chapman, Minnesota-Duluth, Brigham Young, Simon Fraser, Puget Sound, U.C.L.A., New Mexico, Colorado State, the Colorado School of Mines. The School of Mines has men's and women's club teams—the Orediggers and the Lady Orediggers.

When lacrosse players finish college, their options have been even more narrow than the prospects for seniors in high school. Like not a few college ice-hockey players, lacrosse players want to go on playing the game until they qualify for Social Security. In lacrosse for many years, the game's great graduate players concentrated themselves on a single team, which was not inconvenient, since so many of them were neighbors. They were the Mount Washington Lacrosse Club, of Baltimore, and their schedule included not only the best college teams in Baltimoria but all through the East. The annals of big-time college teams are studded with phrases like "did not lose a collegiate game" and "undefeated in collegiate play." It's another way of spelling "Mount Washington." In his three national-championship years coaching Hopkins, Howdy Myers lost to Mount Washington three times and to no one else once. He went on to Hofstra and lost four straight to Mount Washington there.

Jimmy Brown said, some years ago, "When I played, I never saw another black player. The great black athletes wanted to get into the money sports." The great white lacrosse players suiting up in Mount Washington were completely dedicated to a sport that was penniless. They were the virtual professionals in a game that had no professionals. It does now, of course—low-paid moonlighters in six cities (Bayhawks, Cannons, Outlaws, Lizards . . .). To attend some of their games is to go into a time-warp factor. You're on an open field with a small grandstand that could be beside a modest high school. Summer-night lights. Moths in the lights. Everything seems like yesteryear, except the players. Collectively, they are the best ever known, and they are playing in an atmosphere that reminds you of your driver's permit. Matt Danowski (Long Island Lizards) might be playing, or Scott Urick (Washington Bayhawks), or Matt Striebel (Chicago Machine), or John Grant, Jr. (Toronto Nationals). Ryan Boyle, of the Boston Cannons, has a lacrosse I.Q. that is apparently above two hundred. He can see seven passes ahead into a back door that will result in a score. And you might see Sid Smith, of Six Nations, playing for Toronto. At this writing, more than twenty per cent of Toronto's players are Iroquois. The paradoxical and nostalgic milieu that I describe for some of these nascent professional scenes should not be taken generally. Nearly all the outdoor professionals agree that the best home stadium of any team in their league is Denver's Invesco Field at Mile High.

College Park, early summer, and high-school rising seniors from all over the United States have been playing lacrosse all day. And all yesterday. On a pair of fields below the Comcast Center on the vast campus of the University of Maryland. The two fields are parallel and generously fenced—parents not permitted inside the fence. Along the back-to-back sidelines in the blazing sun—in the narrow strip that separates the fields—middle-aged men sit on their personal Renetto Canopy Chairs, or, more commonly, on folding chairs under large golf umbrellas. As they trudge in daily, they resemble caddies, thick elongate bags hanging from their shoulders. Inside the bags are the chairs. The designer chairs are one-piece erections, bag as canopy, canopy as bag. Who else could these people be that they are so prepared? They are college lacrosse coaches. Outnumbering the players playing on the fields beside them, they are from Lehigh, Lynchburg, Trinity, Denver, Virginia, Michigan, Maryland, Moravian, Massachusetts, Princeton, Penn State, Pennsylvania, Providence, North Carolina, Ohio State, Towson, Pace, Washington and Lee, Grand Canyon, Army, Navy, Merchant Marine, Air Force, Eastern Connecticut, Stevens, Siena, Syracuse, Loyola, Lafayette, R.P.I., Randolph-Macon, Bucknell, Cornell, Brown, Dartmouth, Birmingham-Southern, Holy Cross, Colgate, Georgetown, Gettysburg, Rollins, Salisbury, Haverford, Harvard, Hofstra, Hampden-Sydney, Queens, Cabrini, Hobart, Johns Hopkins, Franklin & Marshall, Yale, and Christopher Newport, etcetera. They can swivel in their chairs to watch one game or the other, in sunshine or rain. They carry clipboards, rosters on the clipboards, and mainly they are writing cryptic notes, but bits of conversation now and again float down the midway.

Coach 1: Why did you turn around?

Coach 2: I just wanted to watch Walker Clinton.

Coach 1: Is he good?

Coach 2: No.

Walker Clinton is an invented name, in order to protect the kid who is no good.

Coach 3 to Coach 4: Have you considered Name Withheld?

Coach 4: He has a ninety-seven average but I can't take him. I haven't got room.

Coach 5 to Coach 6: I can't see what he sees in him.

Coach 6: Do not disagree with the man. He hasn't got an opinion unless he's right.

Coach 7 to Coach 8: He has pretty good skills, but he needs serious work in the weight room.

Coach 8: He can't play.

Coach 9: He's probably not going to get it done for us.

Coach 10: I don't think he can play for us, either.

Coach 11: He needs some work stickwise. He's pretty athletic, though. He's tough as shit.

This is like being in a barn at a quarter-horse auction.

Princeton, Towson, and Maryland do not need umbrellas. Princeton, Towson, and Maryland are in a polyethylene pavilion. Their coaches run this camp. When it began, in 1989, it was called Top 205, because two hundred and five high-school players is the number it hoped to attract. It has two overlapping sessions now—each three nights, four days—that draw some eight hundred and eighty high-school players, who are all here on their coaches' recommendations. By N.C.A.A. rule, there can be no "tryout camp," so 205 sends recommendation forms to every high-school lacrosse coach in the country, and the camp must accept, on a first-come first-served basis, anyone who applies. The players want to come because they know who is going to be watching. The guys that resemble caddies are—altogether—about two hundred in number. Princeton's Bill Tierney, winner of multiple national championships and nearing the end of his reign in the East, describes the camp as "one-stop shopping for coaches."

The cryptograms they write to themselves on their roster sheets seem to look upon punctuation as a delay of game.

thick goes hard good skills does too much
clunky
big, athletic, black, rough skills
weak skills, hides
slow good position afraid to engage
no skills, runs away
slow overaggressive dumb
unselfish
selfish solid skills
flashy stick quick burst
good skills too cool?
looks better than he is
looks awkward, gets job done
looks ugly, gets job done
solid athlete, very vanilla
bad athlete
avg athlete lost on field
not horrible

On the first morning, the camp runs one-on-one drills, then half-field scrimmages, then full-field scrimmages, while the camp's own coaches (mainly college assistants) watch. The camp's coaches then pick their teams in a nine-round draft—twenty teams, twenty-two players per team—and these are the units that compete before the visiting buyers.

A kid picks up a ground ball with one hand, saunters toward the crease, and throws a pass away. Fifty coaches write "lazy," or something less flattering.

They very much have in mind the lacrosse I.Q. On a scale from zero to Ryan Boyle, where does a kid register?

    great hands smart
    stone hands dumb
    good skills tough smart
    alert
    not aware
    has a clue
    LH moves well has a clue
    NTB
    slow overaggressive dumb

Sometimes at other lacrosse camps, high-school parents will be seated in grandstands in the presence of college coaches, and maybe looking over the shoulders of coaches at their notes. Tierney hopes they think "NTB" means "not too bad." It means "not too bright." A kid can have 2400 S.A.T.s and a medal from the National Science Foundation and still be not too bright. He moves in a disadvantageous direction. He thinks in the present rather than the future. He "gets mentally in trouble, makes a bad decision with the ball." "LH" means "left-handed."

    good skills dumb dodger
    good vision
    quick dumb w/ball
    good eyes

not bad sees field
good skills athletic understands game

Tierney, on his clipboard, primarily assesses size, speed, and skills. He recognizes four speeds: slow, average, fast, and burner. "A kid can be small if he's fast, but not if he isn't." Size includes huge, midget, meatball, stocky, gross, dumpy, and thick-ass dodger. Among skills are bad stick, average stick, and great stick. "Size, speed, skills—you need two out of three. You can improve stick, but not the other two."

Since the nineteen-eighties, the number of summer lacrosse camps has gone from under forty to more than four hundred. Tuition at the 205 camp is five hundred and ninety-five dollars. The University of Maryland understands math, baking, and how to slice a pie. It feeds the kids nine meals. They sleep in un-air-conditioned dorm rooms, and drag their mattresses into air-conditioned common rooms.

loves to shoot
dumb shooter
good dodger/bad shooter
black hole
tough kid athletic run by anyone bad shooter
black hole, not aware
chucker

A black hole never gives up the ball and a chucker shoots every time he gets the ball.

In 1881, *Harper's Weekly* recalled the near-demise of lacrosse a decade earlier, when "physicians described the dangers of such fast and long-continued running, and anxious parents tried to smother the game in its infancy." Now, at 205 camps, parents wait outside the fence for the arrival of the college coaches and hand them DVDs of their sons' lacrosse highlights. Bill Tierney receives a fair number of DVDs and similar souvenirs ("Are you the Princeton coach?"). "Recruiting is a long-term investment," he says, speaking from his side of the fence. At any given time, he is in contact with six hundred kids—"kids who write us, and kids we write to."

Understanding goalies:

good poise good position
quick hands
not bad stopper
oversteps w/right foot
drops hands on high shot smart talks too much

Players on defense:

very big, athletic, lazy on D
overaggressive
tall thin good slide fast rough
smallish good stick sees field no hustle on D
bad feet
good feet
no feet too much stick
slapper

Three of the many crucial matters in the attack and the mid-field are T&R, no beat, and bag. Like a great open shooter in basketball, if a guy has "time and room," he is going to do something positive. If he is "no beat," he is not going to get past any defender. If he has "bag" written all over him, he has a big sloppy pocket and he throws bad passes.

Appraisals of the offense:

good skills very solid smooth slick hangs perimeter
nifty stick
just catch & finish, no dodge
big good passer, awkward LH shot
slow no shot no dodge
good size quick shots
RH good skills dumb dodger
bad approaches
skinny feeder gets in the way no move
quick moves good vision 2-hander
quick aware fair skills

I cannot resist revealing the name of "quick aware fair skills." From Canandaigua, New York, he is Tom LaCrosse.

good size athletic wants RH no finish
good cutter
athletic tough physical covers ground
LH tough hard nose vg stick
vg off ball
not a ball carrier
good skills LH quick COD
explosive very quick good skills RH sidearm drop
slick in traffic, dances

"COD" is change of direction. "Sidearm drop" is not a large compliment. A lacrosse ball is more likely to end up where the thrower intends it to if his stick goes through a vertical plane. If you lower the stick and wing a sidearm shot, the ball may end up breaking a window somewhere. The great shooters shoot on any plane. Others that imitate them drive their coaches nuts.

In the University of Maryland's Women's Lacrosse and Field Hockey Stadium, under lights in the deep evening of Day Three, twenty-two selected players play against twenty-two other selected players in an All Star game. As it happens, only eight of those stars are from Baltimoria. Six are from Long Island. The high schools of the others are scattered from Connecticut to California, Michigan, Ohio, Georgia, Tennessee. Division I lacrosse coaches are especially attracted by the All Star game. Nearly all the coaches present are standing near the end lines—three times as many coaches as players on the two teams. Sitting in the bleachers are about five hundred other spectators. Some are parents and siblings of the players, but most are campers who were not chosen for the game.

And what a game. Goal answering goal. Fast. Full of isos, inside rolls, two-on-ones, and Gilman clears. Some of the college coaches are far enough along in recruiting talks with some of these high-school stars that they have come to regard them as theirs. A rising senior much in Tierney's field of vision is Forest Sonnenfeldt, who is six feet six, weighs two hundred and forty pounds, and plays in the attack. Among the several things that are unusual about Sonnenfeldt is that he lives and goes to school in New York City. In the geography of lacrosse, says his would-be college coach, "a first-rate player from New York City is something very rare." Sonnenfeldt scores. The other team scores. Sonnenfeldt scores again. He moves well. He is hard to stop. He is "finisher big target RH shooter good skills."

The game will end in a tie and be resolved in overtime. Meanwhile, though, notice big Dave Cottle, head coach of the University of Maryland, who grew up in the row houses of Baltimore, played at Salisbury (on the Eastern Shore), and is one of the five winningest coaches active in the game. As he watches, a rising high-school senior, cradling right-handed, goes into a rocker step, does an inside roll, sprints left, dives headlong, shoots, scores.

Someone says to Dave Cottle, "Is he one of yours?"

And Cottle says, "Not yet."

UNDER THE CLOTH

Under the dark cloth, Laura and Virginia talk. As dialogue goes, it is not memorable.

"Make sure you're happy with the edges."

"Do you want to use the longer lens?"

"The ten-inch is fine."

"The shutter is closed."

"It's cocked."

"Side-to-side level seems fine."

And yet, with luck, the collective effect can sometimes be more than memorable—a single creative photographic leap, done by two people.

They are in there together, bent forward, tandem, looking at the ground glass, their four legs sticking out below the cloth. The image they see is upside down and backward but does not appear that way to them. In their minds, it turns, and flips.

"I like the fact that it's slightly asymmetrical."

"The shape bothers me."

Their own appearance, under the cloth, with the snout of the big camera protruding, is so incongruous and vaudevillian that snapshooters the world over have crowded in to take pictures of Laura and Virginia making pictures.

Their collaborative landscape photography dates from 1987. Everywhere they have been, they have routinely visited botanical gardens, seeking not images but regional insight. They have never made a photograph in such a place, until today.

This is the Bronx in summer, the New York Botanical Garden, the recently renewed Enid A. Haupt Conservatory, and Laura and Virginia are under the dark cloth below the doming center of seventeen thousand panes of glass. They have been attracted by a black circular pool, forty feet across, among jelly palms, saw palmettos, Mexican flags, and crape ferns. The boxlike mahogany camera—a cubic foot and eighteen pounds—inclines toward the water from its tripod to comprehend the reflection of fronds, mullions, clouds, and sky. A visitor—a tourist, a stranger, with a 35-millimetre camera hanging from his neck—comes up politely and asks first if he is in the way, if he is in the picture. To be in the way he would have to be swimming. He has sensed that he is in the presence of an unusual camera but has no idea what it is or what it is looking at. Asking, he asks me, because Laura and Virginia are unavailable under the cloth and mostly out of sight. My expertise in this matter is only marginally greater than his, and derives solely from the fact that Laura is my daughter. When she was in college, I carried these big cameras up more than one pyramid in Yucatán and have been wary of them ever since.

"It's a Deardorff," I say to him. "A view camera—the nineteenth-century, Mathew Brady sort of camera. The negative it makes will be sixty times the size of a negative from yours. The things it captures are amazing. You're O.K., the lens is aimed at the water."

It is not unusual for Laura and Virginia to spend a whole working day driving, walking, looking for images, setting up the camera, fixing its lines with a carpenter's level, chattering under the cloth, making "tilts and swings" and "rises and falls," and not exposing so much as one sheet of film. If they do all that on a given day and open the shutter once, they consider the day successful. They carry a Nikon 35, the sort of camera that most people fire as if it were an automatic weapon, but Laura and Virginia just look through it as if it were a spotting scope, to select and plan images in a preliminary way.

For a couple of hours, they have been staring at the conservatory pool and things are not going well. Subtly, the obsidian water moves. Faint breezes touch it from the open doors and windows. Every three minutes, big misters come on hissing and the vapors stir the air. In their frustration, half an hour ago, Laura and Virginia took the camera down, set it up elsewhere in the building, studied an image, discussed it, spurned it, and returned to the black pool. Under trying conditions, the dialogue within the dark cloth is not wholly technical.

"You should have been a therapist."

"Think so?"

"Yes, but you would not have been able to stop giving advice."

Photographic collaboration tends not to happen, and the list is a short one from Hill and Adamson in the mid-nineteenth century to the married couple Bernd and Hilla Becher of contemporary times. Laura and Virginia, long ago, took two Deardorffs to Iceland, where they intended to use them separately. Laura had first seen Iceland the year before, with me, in pursuit of my work, which had to do with open fissures, a newly risen volcano, moving lava, and the fact that Iceland is a geophysical hot spot coincident at present with the spreading center of the ocean. Its freshly generated landscapes are surreal. Nothing arrested her eye more than the apalhraun—black, jagged, unvegetated plains of rock. She returned to Iceland with Virginia, and they set things up in the apalhraun, and at warm pools with inflatable canoes beside geothermal pumping stations, and in the high winds of Krafla in the interior, where Iceland itself is spreading. Their ideas and subjects were so similar that one of them said, early in the journey, "Maybe we ought to work on this together," and their long collaboration began. Work they did in Iceland is owned by, among other places, the Los Angeles County Museum of Art, the Houston Museum of Fine Arts, and the San Francisco Museum of Modern Art. It has travelled in collected exhibition to Boston, New York, Philadelphia, Detroit, St. Louis, Santiago, Tianjin, London, Prague, Cologne, Basel. Wherever the pictures go, people tend to show bafflement that two photographers can somehow make a single exposure, and they ask how it is done. They ask, over and over again, "Who pressed the button?" And even when they understand that "the button" is the least of it, they tend to remain curious and puzzled. Other artists are full of wonder, too. In Laura's words, "Nobody can believe that two women can go around collaborating for ten years in a field dominated by lone males."

Virginia Beahan and Laura McPhee met in an introductory photography class at Princeton, taught by Emmet Gowin in the fall of 1977. Laura was a sophomore. Virginia, then a high-school English teacher in Pennsylvania, was auditing the course. Laura went on to earn an M.F.A. in photography from the Rhode Island School of Design, and Virginia from the Tyler School of Art. Laura is a professor of photography at the Massachusetts College of Art. Virginia has taught at Mass Art, and also at Harvard, Wellesley, Columbia, and elsewhere. Each works independently as well, and the collaboration may have the future of a teacup resting at the edge of a shelf. Neither one is hesitant with words. In the span of their work together, words by the tens of thousands, in every conceivable category, have been muffled by the dark cloth.

"We work in a kind of shorthand now, after so many years."

"You articulate ideas to each other that you would never articulate to yourself. The collaboration requires the view camera. It forces us to talk about things."

"Our slow intentional way—the way we work—makes it possible for us to collaborate."

These are people whose act takes a long time to get them together. The light is right for them twice a day, and they never choose dawn. An exception once probed the rule, and the exception's name was Sierra Nevada, which rises like a trapdoor and faces east, where the sun never sets. If the Sierra wall is to be seen in raking light, it has to be at dawn. Laura and Virginia saw rusted relics of a nineteen-forties Japanese-American Relocation Center lying in desert sage below the loftiest mountain majesties in the contiguous United States. They got up in the dark, grumbling, fuming, and set up the Deardorff on the fruited plain.

When working in New York or New Jersey, they consistently finish breakfast by noon. At two, they are moving; their day has begun.

"At first, it's frustrating. We look at a lot of stuff, reject most of it, and get depressed."

"Then things start to open up."

A few days ago, they walked in Central Park all afternoon.

"The park is so beautiful and so thought out you feel how every curve and hillock is there for you to get the vistas."

"A lot of what we are looking for is surprise." Bag the park.

They have also been doing rooftops, which require planning.

"This is a new thing for us—arrangements, appointments. We like to be loose."

"New York is a big lotta work."

A roof in the West Twenties was wooden-decked in five levels, had an outdoor shower, a breeze-activated paper goose, a breeze-activated paper loon, concrete dogs, frogs, rabbits, and squirrels, and a rich ecology of real trees, plants, and flowers in sixty tubs, planters, pots, and urns. The roof had teak furniture and had been used as a movie set.

The Empire State Building, a few blocks away, was so immense it was threatening. They turned their backs on it, and let the view camera peer through the vegetation, the wildlife, and twenty-five rooftop water towers spaced out like chessmen to the south.

On a roof close by the western pier of the Brooklyn Bridge, they turned slowly and assessively through an almost circular view: the South Street Seaport ("Tourist agenda"), the Fulton Fish Market ("Funky"), the legendary skyline of lower Manhattan ("Corporate clump").

"The light on the Brooklyn Bridge is soft but dimensional."

"The bridge is so seductive; no matter what you look at, you come back to it."

The camera has various component parts, and to some extent the photographers build it every time they set it up. The lens on its lens board fits into the front standard. The rear standard includes the ground glass—a lightly gridded window exactly the size of the film. The front and rear standards are connected by the accordion-pleated bellows, and all of it rests on the bed, which fits onto the tripod. A system of threaded adjusters gives it more than a little kinship with a surveyor's transit. Aim a 35-millimetre camera up the side of a tall building and the film sees a trapezoid. Fiddle with the knobs on a Deardorff and it sees the building as it is. Tilt the lens a little too much and the edges of the exposure will shade off and become opaque—an effect known as vignetting. L. F. Deardorff & Sons, of Chicago, began making view cameras in the nineteen-twenties. Laura's and Virginia's is forty years old. Its present value is about two thousand dollars. Its lenses cost a thousand dollars apiece. The film costs about ten dollars a sheet.

There were whitecaps on the East River, and once the view camera had been set up, levelled, and adjusted, it tended to wobble in the wind. Although the dark cloth is weighted in its four corners, it flapped while they conferred beneath it.

"Think about color. There's a certain palette here that's hard to break up."

"The white shape in the foreground bothers me."

"Stop. Stop. Go back a touch."

Pleased by what they saw in the ground glass, they stood up side by side, pulled out of the film holder the dark protective slide that covers the film, wrapped the cloth around their shoulders as if they were a pair of living tent poles, opened the shutter for twenty seconds, and successfully shielded the camera from the wind.

You could compile a list of the view camera's burdensome aspects. With the tripod and extra lenses, the whole apparatus weighs more than fifty pounds, and the ground over which they have backpacked it has included sharp lava. Their film travels heavy in a duct-taped Coleman cooler with ice packs wrapped in towels. In addition to dust, Laura and Virginia have seen black flies flying around inside the camera. On a footbridge by the falls in Paterson, New Jersey, the camera shook from pounding water. Heavy traffic vibrates it. To load film, they must be in total darkness. With black-plastic sheets, they blacken the interior of bathrooms. They blacken closets. An entire motel room takes at least an hour. But nothing on the list approaches the challenge of wind.

At Krafla Geothermal Power Station, in Iceland, it was difficult enough for the photographers to remain standing, let alone the bulky camera, in a wind that was bevelling fast-rising steam. Two passing Germans, father and son, helped Laura and Virginia fashion a plastic tent, and the four of them, straining, held off the wind. In Sparanise, in Italy, a wind blew in such concentrated gusts that it stirred blossomed branches in one part of a cherry orchard into cloudlike swirls, while trees close by were motionless, doing the photographers more than a favor. In the middle of Pearl Harbor, they set up the camera on the memorial above the U.S.S. Arizona, but nothing they tried could overcome the wind, and they packed up defeated. ("It was almost as if there were a force that didn't want us to make that picture.") In Sewaren, New Jersey, one January day, they had me along with them so they could show me the true beauty of my native state, and a winter wind was blowing. Their discerning and composing eyes, which had circled the earth, had become strongly attracted to the New Jersey Turnpike, and to the commingled industries and residential enclaves that lie in the flats between the turnpike and the Arthur Kill. On Elf Road, in Sewaren, they found a concrete pier of a railroad overpass that had become a stone monument three stories high, bearing the names of forty-two dead rock stars: Buddy Holly 1959, Big Bopper 1959 . . . Jimi Hendrix 1970, Janis Joplin

1970 . . . Elvis Presley 1977, Keith Moon 1978. . . . In their slow, intentional way, they set up the camera and composed their picture with a deliberation worthy of a great river or of skaters on a Dutch canal, while the object in view of the view camera was an immobile hundred-ton slab. Watching and waiting in that New Jersey wind I found myself thinking, correctly, that I would be far more comfortable if we were doing this in Alaska. New Jersey's wet cold can shrink marrow. The camera on its tripod was shaking like a tree. Much of the waiting was for a moment of relative calm. The moment finally came, and while Laura and Virginia held taut the dark cloth like a shielding banner, Laura counted "a thousand one, a thousand two," and on up as the film took in the light, and she inserted, between counts, gratuitous information for me: "Color film prefers to be overexposed." I prefer not to be and was absorbing nothing.

And now, indoors at the New York Botanical Garden, wind should not be a factor, but even the lightest breath of air can move this nervous water. Twice, they have made exposures that they feel are imperfect. They are far into their third hour, much of it under the cloth, looking for stillness in the shining black reflection. To pass time, I walk around reading the small placards at the bases of trees. I learn that royal palms were named for nothing majestic. Genus *Roystonea*, they were named for Roy Stone. This information fails to entertain Laura or Virginia. After another ten minutes in unacceptable air—with the misters on and the black pool a slightly quivering jelly—Laura says, "I can't deal with this, Virginia; it's driving me insane."

Virginia, reading incident light, has been discussing shutter speeds and f-stops. A Nikon's f-stops stop at 22. This lens goes to 90. Virginia gets back in under the cloth.

Virginia: "I do like the asymmetry."

Laura: "Where is it?"

Virginia: "That's more like what I thought I was seeing."

Laura: "I can't believe we're taking yet another picture of this swamp."

Virginia: "What did you focus on?"

Laura: "The palm at the end of my mind."

The misters, for the moment, turn off. The doors, for the moment, are closed. The air relaxes. You could light a match and the flame would not bend.

"Pull it."

Laura pulls the dark slide.

"Do it."

Virginia moves to open the shutter, but a child near the edge of the pool throws a coin into the water.

Six P.M. on the Mosholu Parkway and in most people's days the equivalent is noon. In this summer light, dusk is still distant, but a faint sense of purpose has come into the air and the professional tempo has abandoned zero. Laura and Virginia taking a picture is analogous to my making notes. Until they see a print, they don't know what they've got. While aiming in a general way at New Jersey, they are reviewing the afternoon's effort and calling it a "scarlet macaw."

In Costa Rica, in the rainy season some years ago, they were finding no images they wanted to take home with them, and day after day passed while conditions failed to improve. Eventually, in their frustration, they set up the Deardorff and tried to make art of a red bird tethered to a stainless-steel tree. This was the one exposure they made in nearly a week. When they looked at the result, they were not surprised by its absolute lack of redeeming value, and the scarlet macaw became for them a symbol for a bad idea resulting in a bad picture.

A voice in the back seat says, "So why don't you give up the Deardorff and settle down with your Hasselblads?"

They shoot back:

"Because of what it sees."

"The quality of description invites slow looking."

"It sees more than the eye would see—a whole view in incredible detail."

"Every hair. Every blade of grass."

From the eighty-square-inch negative, they can achieve that level of detail in a print exceeding forty square feet.

Under the dark cloth, when they look at the ground glass, eight by ten, in effect they are looking at the negative they are making. Much as copilots say to each other, "Wheels down," "Down and locked," Laura and Virginia say repeatedly, "Check the edges of the picture." Do they ever crop?

"Rarely but not never."

"Part of the pleasure of making a picture is getting it right in the frame."

"When you crop it, it's never quite right."

When they study the ground glass under the dark cloth, they are cropping the landscape rather than the picture. They use an eight-power loupe, which looks like a big jeweler's lens, placing it on the ground glass, and looking through it to improve the precision of the focus.

When they count a thousand one, a thousand two, they seem by comparison carefree and vague. Time is as casual as focus is precise. If the light meter suggests four seconds, they'll double it. Thirty seconds—they'll give it a minute. If your lighting of choice is the late, raking kind and the various glooms that follow, you need to give the camera a long slow draught. To exposures of less than a thousandth of a second and exposures of one second or more the photochemical law of reciprocity does not apply. The product of light and time is not constant. Known as reciprocity failure, this phenomenon (or lack of one) tends to detach from technology the photographer who wants to work in low and failing light. Improvisation enters the equation. The procedure goes supple, like an inspired chef tasting everything and measuring nothing.

"It's like salt."

"You throw on a few more grains."

"As we told you, better over than under."

"With color film, underexposed is the kiss of death."

They made a fifteen-minute exposure of an artificial volcano erupting water in Las Vegas. Virginia, all the while, was on patrol, intercepting passersby, trying to prevent them from walking in front of the camera. She failed to see an infiltrating Asian tourist, who reached the camera and stared straight at it from a distance of ten inches. "He's got his nose in our open lens!" Virginia screamed, and ran over to shoo him away. Shutter open, the camera went on looking at the volcano. The exposure was such a long one that the man did not show up in the picture, which belongs to the art museum of Princeton University.

During a twenty-minute exposure at a reservoir in Costa Rica, power boats and windsurfers moved in and out of the picture, but when it was developed they weren't there. During a long exposure over plunging sluices at a reservoir in Sri Lanka, big white ibises flew in and out of the picture, but when it was developed they weren't there.

While Laura and Virginia were making a slow exposure of a chaparral fire in California, a line of prisoners, in orange fire-fighting suits, walked through the picture from left to right but escaped being caught on film.

In the Aeolian Islands, they opened the shutter for an hour and a half on the real Stromboli, erupting. While they waited, they went for pizza. The darkly outlined final product was brightened by motion: by the shifting stars, by the flashlights of hikers, by the ninety-minute brushstroke of the moon.

They cross the George Washington Bridge to New Jersey and go north on the Palisades Parkway to Rockefeller Lookout in Englewood Cliffs. From the river the rise is sheer, two hundred feet, to the brink where they set up the camera, after climbing over a protective fence. This is one of the New York views that belongs in Category 1 with the view over the water from the Staten Island Ferry near Richmond and the view from the summit of the Throgs Neck Bridge. Past the Bronx and Yonkers, the reach upriver extends at least twenty miles. Directly opposite, the drawbridge is open in the Spuyten Duyvil, stopping the toy trains. Downriver, the great bridge brackets the receding city—Morningside and midtown and the Village valley and Wall Street. What they see in the ground glass is a fifty-fifty ratio of concentrated city and tree-covered diabase-palisade cliffs, with a fjord running through. In their constant search for the dividing lines between altered and unaltered worlds, this scene is at mid-spectrum.

The river lies on a fault, I contribute. The rock on the two sides is in all respects different, and the New York side is a billion years older. With loupe and level, Laura and Virginia are speeding up. On the cliffside, the falling light has turned half of the crown of one young maple gold. "We're going to lose that in about a minute—that tree. We're going to lose that light." They let the camera soak it in for three minutes. Virginia, as she waits, expresses some regret that the film is not Fuji. It is Kodak Vericolor, which she says is "very natural," but she mentions "the acid green of Fuji," and its "intense saturation of color." Looking down the river at the city, she adds, "A soft shot like this, the Fuji might juice it up."

We drift south, toward Jersey City, for a rendezvous at sunset with the Colgate clock. Funded by foundation grants, their pictures are from Iceland, Costa Rica, Hawaii, Sri Lanka, southern Italy, southern California. Why New Jersey?

"We both grew up near Trenton."

"It's a landscape with the aspect of memory."

In Trenton, the Deardorff spent ten evening minutes drinking in the Bridge Street bridge. Anyone who grew up near Trenton, as I did, too, will accord that bridge the aspect of memory, with its bathetic letters that all but span the Delaware:

TRENTON MAKES   THE WORLD TAKES

The long exposure glossed the river, turned it into delinear frosting.

The allure for them of Carteret and Rahway is shared, safe to say, by no one else passing through on the turnpike, but they see in its refinery tanks and residential streets a "fantastic landscape"—in a phantasmagorical sense "a landscape of dreams."

They even compare Carteret to Hawaii. In the lava fields of Kilauea, among the record outpourings of recent times, are isolated parcels of spared ground called kipukas—a few acres, here and there, that the lava has so far missed. On some of these are surviving houses with people still in them. Instinctively, Laura and Virginia were drawn off the turnpike and into the kipukas of Carteret, where bungalows with picket fences survive the industrial magma.

"People are in a place."

"The place changes around them."

"They don't leave."

One summer evening, parked at such a place, they were waiting out a thunderstorm and planning a picture that would include both the pickets and the Port Reading Refinery. As they studied the background, a bolt of lightning came down through it and a huge black cloud shot to the sky. The lightning had ignited three million gallons of gasoline. While the black smoke roiled overhead, they made their picture.

The Colgate clock is half a mile south of the Holland Tunnel beside the slip of a ferry to Manhattan. The view across the water to Wall Street is, easily, in Category 1, and now, at 8 P.M., a hundred thousand Wall Street windows are glistening copper. The sun is so low over New Jersey that its westward-raking light must be feeling for Hokkaido. Its easterly rays backlight the big clock through a frieze of rooftops, tree crowns, razor wire, and chain link, described by these photographers as "a tableau of urban living." Like a Ferris wheel, the clock is an open, skeletal structure—an octagonal analog timepiece with hands thirty feet long. As dusk arrives, the hands are illuminated in red neon. Hours are represented not by numbers but by red neon streaks, and the whole two-thousand-square-foot face is surrounded by rows of white lightbulbs.

Laura and Virginia have climbed a chain-link fence and set up the Deardorff on a crumbling slab of old pier. Three steps backward and they're in the river. Pressure rises. Police could break this up. The sun is vanishing fast. On this July night, the wind off the water is surprisingly cold. But the clock itself is the principal agent of today's crepuscular crescendo. They have chosen 8:20 as the optimum moment for opening the shutter, because of the drooping dihedral of the illuminated hands.

To lift the lens above the fence line, the tripod is fully extended, and one at a time they have to get up on the camera's storage box to see what is under the dark cloth. A ferry docks, and people walk by grinning.

"We have vignetting."

"Can we frame it differently?"

"All I want is to make sure we get an eight-by-ten out of this."

"With the vignetting we're in trouble."

"Maybe we'll like it."

"We need to level side to side."

Eight-fifteen P.M. "Cool. We're going to be right on schedule."

"I think this is going to be beautiful."

"I'm so happy for you."

Shivering, the two of them wrap themselves in the dark cloth. Virginia, standing on the camera box, removes the slide, and steps down.

"What do we want to do?"

"Three minutes."

"O.K., three minutes."

"Pull it."

"Check the wind."

They unwrap themselves, open the shutter, and for three minutes hold up the cloth against the wind. During the three minutes, a man and a woman, dressed Wall Street and approaching the ferry, walk right into the picture.

"It's O.K."

"They won't register on the film."

Now the man and the woman slow down—in front of the camera, in front of the fifty-foot clock—and each one is tapping at a phone.

Slowly, they leave the picture, with a full minute to go.

"So there was a piece I was reading last night about a couple who wrote together and about the terrors of collaboration."

"So they got divorced?"

"They discovered that two heads are better than one."

MY LIFE LIST

My life list is in no way comparable to Sandy Frazier's, and I hope that anyone reading this will not even faintly imagine that I am presuming otherwise as I go on to mention my own modest history with eccentric food. In this field, Sandy is an idol—certainly my idol, probably your idol. He it was who improved his understanding of wild trout by filling his belly with brown-drake mayflies, chewing thoughtfully while they fluttered on his tongue ("If you're into mayflies, it's hard to eat just one"). He it is whose acquired tastes run to things like grasshopper juice and cricket thighs ("the feel of the cricket's toothpicky legs between my teeth"). A gift of chocolate-covered ants and bees appealed to him less for the chocolate than for the "chitinous crunch." Long known in *The New Yorker* as Ian, a name unfairly thought to be a sign of personal aggrandizement, he reads Leviticus for the sheer pleasure of its culinary attention to "unclean creeping things." That phrase belongs, Lord knows, to Leviticus, for it could never be from Sandy, who is incapable of writing such a description of anything, anywhere, that can qualify as protein.

I am simply not in his league, and prefer my place on the sidelines, admiring what I see. I mean, yes, when I was eight years old in the Vermont fish hatchery I used to swallow little two-inch whole trout—toss them high in the air and stagger around under them and catch them wriggling in my open mouth—but I never reached the point of eventual development implied by that early promise. When Sandy eats something that you don't find at ShopRite, at least not for sale at ShopRite, he does it for the art of it—in his word, the "show" of it—while I only do it for a living. I've eaten things like dock, burdock, chicory, chickweed, snapper eggs, porpoise, and mountain oysters, but almost always in the line of duty—on-the-job consumption. If I am out working and some novel thing is set in front of me, I'll eat it. But some novel thing is not often set in front of me, which is one reason that I defer so completely and uncompetitively to Sandy's amazing record, beside which I'd have little to show but several pounds of grizzly bear.

Its taxonomic name is *Ursus horribilis*, but that, for sure, is not how it tastes. About thirty years ago in Alaska in early spring, Mike Potts, a trapper, asked me to help him write a brochure for dogsled trips he wanted to sell to tourists from the Lower Forty-eight. Since I wouldn't take his money (in part because he had none), he paid me in food. One evening, the fare included fresh shoulder of grizzly, fried in its own raging fat by his wife, Adeline, and set on a table in their cabin, in Eagle Indian Village. A couple of days earlier, Potts and another trapper had been on the Fortymile River, and returned to Eagle by canoe, a journey that took them out of Alaska and into Yukon Territory and back into Alaska on the Yukon River.

The bear was walking upwind, downriver, looking the other way—just on the Canadian side of the border. The two raised their rifles, fired, and knocked it into the United States. Halved at the waist, it has been hanging in Potts' butchery, a few steps from his cabin. . . . Burgundy is the color of the grizzly's flesh. With the coat gone, its body is an awesome show of muscular anatomy. The torso hangs like an Eisenhower jacket, short in the middle, long in the arms, muscles braided and bulging. The claws and cuffs are still there. A great deal of fat is on the back. The legs, still joined, suggest a middle linebacker, although the thought is flattering to football.

Adeline would not eat the *shar-cho*—in Hungwitchin (her language), the brown, or grizzly, bear.

She will eat lynx, she said, which is "just like turkey," and wolf, which recalls canned beef. But not this, never this meat. There might be taste but there was terror in the bear.

Adeline cooked a platter of moose and set it on the table beside a platter of bear—two large mounds of sliced meat at least eight inches high. In addition to the three of us, a couple of other people were present. You reached for the meat with your own fork. Steadily, the pile of grizzly meat diminished, not so the moose.

The moose was tough. I ate little of it. The grizzly was tender with youth and from a winter in the den. More flavorful than any wild meat I have eaten, it expanded my life list—muskrat, weasel, deer, moose, musk ox, Dall sheep, whale, lion, coachwhip, rattlesnake . . . grizzly. And now a difference overcame me with regard to bears. In strange communion, I had chewed the flag,

consumed the symbol of the total wild, and, from that meal forward, if a bear should ever wish to reciprocate, it would only be
what I deserve.

The rattlesnake was canned. The flag of Alaska is dark blue
behind gold stars that form the constellation of the Great Bear.

Soon after the Alaska Native Claims Settlement Act was
passed, in 1971, which resulted in the reorganization of Alaskan
land on a vast and complex scale, I developed a strong desire to
go there, stay there, and write about the state in its transition.
When I asked William Shawn, The New Yorker's editor, if he would
approve and underwrite the project, his response was firm and
negative. Why? Not because it was an unworthy subject, not
because The New Yorker was over budget, but because he didn't
want to read about any place that cold. He had a similar reaction
to Newfoundland ("Um, uh, well, uh, is it cold there?"). Newfoundland, like Florida, is more than a thousand miles below the
Arctic Circle, but Mr. Shawn shivered at the thought of it. I never
went to work in Newfoundland, but, like slowly dripping water, I
kept mentioning Alaska until at last I was in Chicago boarding
Northwest 3.

The first long river trip I made up there was on the Salmon
and the Kobuk, on the south slope of the Brooks Range. At
some point, I learned and noted that the forest Eskimos of that
region valued as a great delicacy the fat behind a caribou's eye.
Pat Pourchot, of the federal Bureau of Outdoor Recreation (in
recent years Alaska's commissioner of natural resources), had organized the river trip and collected the provisions. Pourchot's
fields of special knowledge did not include food. For breakfast, he
brought along a large supply of Pop-Tarts encrusted in pink icing

and filled with raspberry jam. This caused me, in the manuscript ultimately delivered to the magazine, to present from the banks of the Kobuk River a philosophical choice:

> Lacking a toaster, and not caring much anyway, we eat them cold. They invite a question. To a palate without bias—the palate of an open-minded Berber, the palate of a travelling Martian—which would be the more acceptable, a pink-icinged Pop-Tart with raspberry filling (cold) or the fat gob from behind a caribou's eye?

There was in those days something known as "the Shawn proof." From fact-checkers, other editors, and usage geniuses known as "readers," there were plenty of proofs, but this austere one stood alone and seldom had much on it, just isolated notations of gravest concern to Mr. Shawn. If he had an aversion to cold places, it was as nothing beside his squeamishness in the virtual or actual presence of uncommon food. I had little experience with him in restaurants, but when I did go to a restaurant with him his choice of entrée ran to cornflakes. He seemed to look over his serving flake by flake to see if any were moving. On the Shawn proof, beside the words quoted above, he had written in the wide, white margin—in the tiny letters of his fine script—"the pop tart."

So I have no idea by what freakishness of inattention Mr. Shawn had approved my application, a few years earlier, to go around rural Georgia with a woman who collected, and in many cases ate, animals dead on the road. She actually had several agendas, foremost of which was that she—Carol Ruckdeschel—and her colleague Sam Candler in the Georgia Natural Areas Council were covering the state in quest of wild acreages that might be preserved before it was too late. Under this ecological fog, Mr. Shawn seems not to have noticed the dead animals, let alone thought of them as anybody's food, but I was acutely conscious from Day One of the journey and Day One of the writing that my first and perhaps only reader was going to be William Shawn. It shaped the structure, let me tell you. Where to begin? With the weasel we ate the first night out? Are you kidding, I asked myself, and did not need to wait for the answer. This was an episodic narrative of eleven hundred miles—embracing an isolated valley in the Appalachian north and Cemocheckobee Creek, in the far south—and I could start in the shrewdest possible place in a structure to be shaped like a nautilus by chronological flashback. Where to begin? Near Hunger and Hardship Creek, on the Swainsboro Road, in Emanuel County, we had come upon a dying turtle—a snapping turtle. There had been a funny scene with a sheriff who tried to shoot the turtle at point-blank range and missed. A turtle is not a weasel. Snapping turtles are not unknown to commercial soupmakers. Weighing a snapping turtle against weasels and water moccasins did not require consultation. The scene on the trip that had followed the turtle was a stream-channelization project—no food for squeamishness there. And after the turtle and the channelization I could go off into the biography of the central figure (Carol Ruckdeschel) and I'd have managed what turned out to be eight thousand words of a Shawn-wise beginning before I had to start over and eat that weasel.

I turned in the manuscript and went for a five-day walk in my own living room. The phone rang.

"Hello."

"Hello, Mr. McPhee. How are you?" He spoke in a very light, very low, and rather lilting voice, not a weak voice, but diffident to a spectacular extent for a man we called the iron mouse.

"Fine, thank you, Mr. Shawn. How are you?"

"Fine, thank you. Is this a good time to be calling?"

"Oh, yes."

"Well, I liked your story . . . No. I didn't like your story. I could hardly read it. But that woman is closer to the earth than I am. Her work is significant. I'm pleased to publish it."

Carol measured the weasel. She traced him on paper and fondled his ears. His skull and skin would go into the university's research collection.

As a research biologist, she gathered skulls and pelts for Georgia State University, whose students in their labs wore them out so quickly that they needed frequent replacement.

With a simple slice, she brought out a testicle; she placed it on a sheet of paper and measured it. Three-quarters of an inch. Slicing smoothly through the weasel's fur, she began to remove the pelt. Surely, she worked the skin away from the long neck. The flesh inside the pelt looked like a segment of veal tenderloin. "I lived on squirrel last winter," she said. "Every time you'd come to a turn in the road, there was another squirrel. I stopped buying meat. I haven't bought any meat in a year, except for some tongue. I do love tongue." While she talked, the blade moved in light, definite touches. "Isn't he in perfect shape?" she said. "He was hardly touched. You really lose your orientation when you start skinning an animal that's been run over by a Mack truck."

"Fine, thank you, Mr. Shawn. How are you?"

Carol put the weasel on the tines of a long fork and roasted it over the coals. "How do you like your weasel?" Sam asked me. "Extremely well done," I said. Carol sniffed the aroma of the roast. "It has a wild odor," she said. "You *know* it's not cow. The first time I had bear, people said, 'Cut the fat off. That's where the bad taste is.' I did, and the bear tasted just like cow. The next bear, I left the fat on." The taste of the weasel was strong and not unpleasant. It lingered in the mouth after dinner. The meat was fibrous and dark.

A reading from the Book of Leviticus, the eleventh chapter, verses 1–3: "And the Lord spake unto Moses and to Aaron, saying unto them, Speak unto the children of Israel, saying, These are the beasts which ye shall eat among all the beasts that are on the earth. Whatsoever parteth the hoof, and is clovenfooted, and cheweth the cud, among the beasts, that shall ye eat." 20–23: "All fowls that creep, going upon all four, shall be an abomination unto you. Yet these may ye eat of every flying creeping thing that goeth upon all four, which have legs above their feet, to leap withal upon the earth; Even these of them ye may eat; the locust after his kind, and the bald locust after his kind, and the beetle after his kind, and the grasshopper after his kind. But all other flying creeping things, which have four feet, shall be an abomination unto you." 29–30: "These also shall be unclean unto you among the creeping things that creep upon the earth; the weasel, and the mouse, and the tortoise after his kind, and the ferret, and the chameleon, and the lizard, and the snail, and the mole."

No one west of Hoboken needs to be told what mountain oysters are, least of all Scott Davis, a Union Pacific engineer, who was driving not a train but his Suburban when the subject came up between us, east of the Laramie Range. We were on our way through falling snow to Bill, Wyoming, to catch a coal train to Black Thunder Mine, and Scott said he was sort of hungry for mountain oysters. He knew a place in Douglas where we could get them. It had been a while since his last testicle.

I must have been telling him about Chris Collis, a Nevada brand inspector whose work I had once described, and about an evening I spent with Chris and his family in a small mountain valley above seven thousand feet, where the Collises kept sixty-seven head of their own cattle. Chris, Karen, and their children—Christopher, Gerry, and Eleni—were there to round up and brand calves. Watching them from a corral fence, I scribbled notes:

> Full-blood Saler bull calf, roped on one hind leg, screaming. Dad lifts him, flips him, marks his ears. He slices off the tip of the scrotum as if he were scissoring the tip of a cigar. He squeezes into the light the pearl-gray glistening ellipsoid oysters. He does not cut the cords but works them with the blade—scraping, shaving, thinning until they part. The process greatly reduces loss of blood. The calf's eyeballs, having rotated backwards, are two-

thirds white. . . . "Who's going to eat the oysters?" Christopher says. Calf No. 6 is also a bull. These are not young calves, and they are hard to hold. They weigh at least three hundred pounds. At last, this one is stretched out, bawling, tongue protruding far, eyeballs largely white. From the bunched animals across the corral a cow emerges, boldly approaches the people and the prostrate calf, and smells it. Identification positive. He is hers. She goes on snuffling him but does not become aggressive. "Some cows would try to hook or butt you," Chris remarks. Six-year-old Eleni . . . is holding the vaccination gun and the antiseptic spray. "Get behind him," her father tells her, accepting the vaccine. He tries to hand her the oysters. She says firmly, "I don't want 'em." Soon Gerry is carrying a cup of oysters. Hereabouts, they appear on menus as entrées. "They are real rich, like sweetbreads," Chris says. "You've probably had mountain oysters before. You cook them in a Dutch oven. You brown them in oil and garlic, and bake them. They are also called fries."

At the Plains Restaurant, in Douglas, Wyoming, they were called mountain oysters. You would not compare them to Teuscher *truffes*. They looked, however, like a generous plateful of filled chocolates that had been left out in the sun. They met Scott's expectations, and, actually, mine. Taste like? They tasted like mountain oysters. If I were forced to compare them to a common food, I would call them grilled macho chicken hearts. I did not get up from the table prepared to screw my weight in wildcats.

After a research trip to the Vestmann Islands, in Iceland, I brought two puffins through U.S. customs at Newark. They weighed down my suitcase, but declaring them slipped my mind. One puffin was fresh, the other had been smoked. I bought them in a grocery store on Heimaey (hay-may), an island about seven miles off Iceland's south coast. Puffins are regarded as adorable birds, and I am not unmindful of the hostile correspondence this story could arouse. But, stranger, stay thy hand. Iceland has more puffins than Frank Perdue had chickens in his lifetime. There are a million puffins in the Vestmann Islands alone.

Islanders collect puffin eggs by belaying down the faces of sheer high cliffs and filling baskets. When they collect living puffins, they are sitting in niches or hanging from ropes as well. They eat them smoked, salted, boiled, or fried. Pall Helgason, of Heimaey, said, "Puffins, women, and wine are alike. The older they grow, the better they taste." A fisherman in the harbor told me that he roasts his puffins for one hour, turns the oven off, and removes the puffin thirty minutes later. He also boils puffins in salt water—a two-hour simmer with the lid on. Hot on my plate one evening at the Hotel Gestgjafinn were three smoked puffin breasts—dark brown, smooth, and leathery. They were as red as wine inside. Their taste was an almost exact cross between corned beef and kippered herring. They were served with large cubes of butter, boiled small potatoes, and thin slices of sweet pickle.

Not many years before, a long fissure had suddenly opened on Heimaey, running through grazing land, low and flat, and pouring forth incandescent lava. Before long, a volcano stood there—seven hundred feet high. The lavas that produced it spread over farms and into town and threatened to enter and destroy Iceland's most important fishing harbor. The nation fought the lava with fire hoses, saving the harbor. The lava deeply buried or otherwise obliterated two hundred buildings.

Under the lava is Olafshus, home of the late Erlendur Jonsson, master catcher of puffins. Olafshus had territorial rights to Alfsey, which is two miles from Heimaey. He and a crew of three or four sat in high niches in the dizzying cliffs of Alfsey, and with long-handled nets caught puffins in flight. In a four-week season, Erlendur would be content if he returned to Olafshus, and his wife, Olafia, with twelve thousand puffins. Olafshus went very quickly under the lava. The puffin is among the nation's emblematic birds. With its bright-white chest, its orange webbed feet, and its big orange scimitar bill, it could be an iced toucan.

From Alaska, I flew to Newark with moose meat one time—actually, mooseburger, given to me in a five-pound block by Ed and Ginny Gelvin, who lived in Central, about a hundred miles northeast of Fairbanks. They had raised their children on moose, and used it in just about every form in which "Joy of Cooking" calls for beef. Our own children were young and, in those days, were on the approximate level of William Shawn as venturesome eaters. The solution to this problem was simple. I shaped the moose meat into patties, grilled them over charcoal, and set them on the table without comment.

Once, also, I took a Yukon River king salmon—a forty-pound chinook—out of Jim Scott's gill net in the eddy under Eagle Bluff, wondering if I could get it to New Jersey in an edible state. We froze it whole in Jim's freezer in Eagle, and it stayed there long enough to get pretty far up the mineral-hardness scale. On the morning when the mail plane was coming and would take me away, we wrapped the big king in enough insulation material to make it look like some sort of mummy. The month was July. The Fahrenheit temperature, in this hottest and coldest region of Alaska, was in the seventies. The mail plane, a Cessna, showed up. I put the fish in it and flew to Fairbanks, two hundred miles. Because I wasn't leaving Fairbanks for a day or two, I took the fish to a restaurant and checked it in to the restaurant's freezer. The itinerary from Fairbanks to Newark was in two parts— overnight to Sea-Tac and an early-morning plane east. The salmon went as checked baggage. In Newark, I waited by the baggage rack, and waited, and at last the king salmon appeared among the suitcases. I did not inspect it. Outside the terminal, the temperature was above ninety. You could drink the air. I had been met by my wife, Yolanda, and we put the fish in the car and drove the forty miles home. In the stifling heat of our back hall (my middle initial, A., does not stand for air-conditioning), I unrolled the many layers of Jim Scott's insulation. The fish hit the floor and damned near cracked the bricks. It was as hard as granite. We made gravlax.

I should finish the story about the mooseburger. The kids ate it without comment, their gentle chatter focussed on their usual weighty topics. When they reached for more burgers, I told them they were eating an Alaskan moose. "Eeeeeeee!" "Uhhhhhhh!" "Gross!" "Disgusting!" A few of them still talk to me.

The longest time I ever lived on foraged wild food came about in this manner: While I was in college, I was the left-handed catcher on a summer softball team that represented the Gallup Poll. Joshua L. Miner III, our shortstop, was a local schoolteacher who later taught at Gordonstoun, in Scotland, and returned to the United States bringing Outward Bound with him. He was its original American director. His first two Outward Bound schools were set up in Colorado and Minnesota, then he added one on Hurricane Island, in Maine. I went there with him to scout the scene for a possible piece for *The New Yorker*, and among the people Josh introduced me to was Euell Gibbons, who was teaching students how to survive on nothing but foraged foods—not a particularly large challenge in summer on an island in Penobscot Bay. Back in the office in New York, I asked to see Mr. Shawn, and went in and told him about my visit to the island, and proposed a long fact piece on the Outward Bound movement. He said, slowly and politely, "Oh." After a time, he added, "Oh, that would not be for us." He said Outward Bound reminded him of Hitler Youth. Gibbons, though, sounded interesting. Why not just go off somewhere— somewhere other than Outward Bound—with Euell Gibbons, and do a profile of him? The fact that Gibbons wrote about edible wild vegetation to the exclusion of almost all animal tissue but blue-eyed scallops had not been lost on Mr. Shawn. So, in mid-November, 1966, I went off with Gibbons from his home in Troxelville, Pennsylvania, and spent nearly a week canoeing down the Susquehanna River, backpacking on the Appalachian Trail, and living on dock, burdock, chicory, chickweed, ground-cherries, groundnuts, dandelions, and oyster mushrooms, among many other things we foraged. For me, as a survivor on wild food, that personal best was only a few days. Euell, in an earlier phase of his life, had lived exclusively on foraged food for three years.

For dinner on the first night—beside the river, blowing white streams of breath—we consumed boiled whole dandelions, boiled Jerusalem artichokes, ground-cherry salad, and pennyroyal tea. The dandelions were on the old side and tough. The ground-cherries, of the nightshade family, seemed to me to have "the flavor of tomatoes, with a wild, musky undertone."

Gibbons: "These things are not substitutes for tame foods. They have flavors of their own, and it is not fair to them to call them by the name of something else."

"Jerusalem," in this context, was a corruption of the Italian *girasole*.

Gibbons: "These are not artichokes. They're sunflower tubers."

With a knife and fork, he laid one open and then scooped up a mound of the white flesh. It was steaming hot. "Boy!" he said. "That goes down very gratefully. Just eating greens, you can get awfully damn hungry. We'll eat plenty of greens, but we need these, too."

For breakfast, we had watercress, cattail sprouts, chicory greens, burdock roots, persimmons, and water-mint tea.

He warned me that breakfast is the roughest meal to get through on any survival trip, because that is usually the time when the wild foods are most dissimilar from the foods one is used to at home.

For our first lunch, lying on a gravel bar, we had had walnuts, hickory nuts, and persimmons. For our second lunch, on the shore of a big island, we had walnuts, hickory nuts, watercress, and persimmons.

Like people in all parts of the country, we were eating essentially the same lunch we had had the day before, and it was not much of a thrill.

Before dinner, we had catnip tea.

He said that catnip is a mild sedative, and I drank all I could hold.

Then, in addition to dandelions, we ate oyster mushrooms, big as saucers. Thick, steaming, and delicious, they had the aroma of oyster stew and the taste of grilled steak. Or so it seemed. In the morning, foraging a few hundred yards from the river, we found a patch of ground that a farmer's plow could not reach because of a bend in a very small stream. On that fifth of an acre, we found wild mustard, lamb's-quarters, chickweed, wild spearmint, catnip, winter cress, groundnuts, and off-the-scale dandelions.

"This is the best dandelion field I've ever got into," he said as he pried one after another out of the earth. "I've seen *cultivated* dandelions that weren't as big as this!"

Lunch: boiled dandelion crowns, walnuts, and catnip tea sweetened with sugar. He had made the sugar eight months before, in Troxelville, and we had brought it with us intending— after the first couple of days—to introduce condiments into our diet, one per meal.

"I've made sugar from the sap of red maples, silver maples, Norway maples—hell, yes—and from walnut trees, butternut trees, sycamores, black birches. This? This is sugar-maple sugar. This is living."

After stashing the canoe and heading south from Clarks Ferry on the Appalachian Trail, we spent the night at a lean-to shelter, where we introduced vegetable oil.

The night was going to be clear and cold, and we kept the fire high. By seven, when Gibbons had the two frying pans out and was beginning to sauté dandelion roots in one and sliced groundnuts in the other, the temperature at the open end of the lean-to was below freezing and the temperature at the closed end was almost a hundred degrees. The distance between these extremes was eight feet. Gibbons seemed at home there, cooking, with his face baking and his back freezing, and the dinner he served was outstanding—wild-spearmint tea, piles of crisp dandelion-root tidbits, and great quantities of groundnuts so skillfully done that they seemed to be a refinement of home-fried potatoes. Having fried food was an appealing novelty. We were hungry, and we ate as rapidly as Nilotic tribesmen, without conversing. Gibbons looked up once and said, "The Smithsonian has a very good man on starchy roots." Then he went on eating.

After the coldest night I have ever spent anywhere, below or above the Arctic Circle, we sustained ourselves on wintergreen berries, winter cress, mallow cheeses, wintergreen tea. Witch-hazel tea. White-pine-needle tea.

It had in its taste the tonic qualities of the scent of pine, but it was not at all bitter. I had imagined, on first trying it the night before, that I would have a feeling I was drinking turpentine. Instead, I had had the novel experience of an unfamiliar taste that was related to a completely familiar scent—a kind of direct translation from one idiom to another.

My daughters consider me the least observant person they know ("A rhinoceros could walk through the living room and he wouldn't notice it")—a claim that is not unsupported by the fact that I have never seen a rattlesnake in the wild. In Western states for forty-odd years I have been going into rattlesnake terrain and not seen one. I have slept on their ground. I have walked ridges where I was told to step carefully because rattlesnakes would be everywhere like earthworms after rain. With a sedimentologist, I went up a trail to an outcrop in Iowa past a sign that said "EXPECT TO SEE RATTLESNAKES." No apparent rattlesnakes. In Atlanta, I shared a room with Carol Ruckdeschel's young diamondback rattlesnake, Zebra, but he was living in a big jar and didn't count. On Cumberland Island, off the Georgia coast, Sam Candler, who has spent much of his life there, was telling me one day about having discovered a timber rattler under the driver's seat of his Jeep. The Jeep was in motion when he made the discovery and he was the driver. The rattlesnakes of Cumberland Island are thicker than fire hoses and so numerous they're like earthworms after rain. So I'm told. I told Sam that I had yet to see my first rattler in the wild. "You what?" he said, pulling his beard in disbelief. "You can't be serious."

"I'm serious."

"Well," he said, "let's go!" We went outside and got into his Jeep. I looked it over first. Sam knows the name and address of every rattlesnake in the northern five thousand acres of the island. He tells stories unflattering to their intelligence: "If a line of people walks past a rattlesnake, it aims at the first person, strikes at the second, and hits the third." He stopped near a stand of palmettos, walked confidently to the edge of it, and peered in. Nobody home. Near an immense live oak, he showed confidence again. No snake. We drove around for a couple of hours, frequently stopping at rattlesnake loci familiar to him for a lifetime. His confidence ebbed and was replaced by amazement.

The Rocky Mountain geologist David Love, who generously made field trips with me and camped with me and taught me the structure and stratigraphy of Wyoming, was no less surprised than Sam Candler. David had grown up in the geographical center of the state on a ranch from which no other buildings were visible to the distant horizons. A man named Bill Grace, wanted for murder, had come through the ranch one evening when David and his brother were young boys. Their parents knew who Grace was, and did not think ill of him for killing a man who had it coming to him. The boys knew that Grace was wanted for murder. Their mother asked him to stay for dinner. The boys happened to have come upon and killed a five-foot rattlesnake earlier in the day. Their mother served it creamed on toast. The boys were cautioned sternly by their parents not to use the word "rattlesnake" at any point during the meal.

They were to refer to it as chicken, since a possibility existed that Bill Grace might not be an eater of adequate sophistication to enjoy the truth. The excitement was too much for the boys. Despite the parental injunction, gradually their conversation at the table fished its way toward the snake. Casually—while the meal was going down—the boys raised the subject of poisonous vipers, gave their estimates of the contents of local dens, told stories of snake encounters, and so forth. Finally, one of them remarked on how very good rattlers were to eat.

Bill Grace said, "By God, if anybody ever gave me rattlesnake meat I'd kill them."

The boys went into a state of catatonic paralysis. In the pure silence, their mother said, "More chicken, Bill?"

"Don't mind if I do," said Bill Grace.

My life list of exotic food is not something I feel compelled to increase. I have no kinship with list-conscious birders who get into their vans and drive round-the-clock because someone somewhere has sighted an endangered warbler. I simply do not think like that. So I ate ostrich at the 1906 Restaurant, in Callicoon, New York. So what? Ostrich is a specialty there, and it's arterially correct. So I stretched the list a little by eating cow tendons, fermented white soybeans, fermented black soybeans, stewed conch, sea cucumbers, and durian at my friend Andrew Co's Sakura Express, on Witherspoon Street in my home town. So what? Durian, also known as monthong, is a fruit that smells strongly fecal and tastes like tiramisu. Sea cucumber, the holothurian echinoderm, has a muscular body and an extensive respiratory tree that soften deliciously in steam, becoming somewhat gelatinous and not unlike ox marrow. I ate lion and whale when I was nineteen years old on separate visits to Keen's English Chop House, on Thirty-sixth Street. I was gathering experience. Betsy Candler, whose husband is Sam, cooked porpoise one time and withheld its identity until she had asked what I thought I was eating. I said, "Whale." On another occasion, when she grilled a coachwhip, I didn't know it from a corn snake. Under cross-examination, though, I would have to admit that certain terminal frustrations may have come into play when I went into a restaurant in Denver not long ago and ordered rattlesnake. Buckhorn Exchange, 1000 Osage Street—on the walls enough stuffed heads to make a quorum in the House of Representatives. I was with grandchildren and I still have the check: "6 sarsaparilla. 1 rattlesnake."

Monica Wojcik, an '07 Princeton graduate who, in her senior year, ran the Boston Marathon and, with her mother, the San Francisco Marathon, once gave me a drink of bee spit before we went off on a sixteen-mile bike ride. She called it bee spit but it was actually synthetic hornet juice—Vaam brand, available only in Japan. Liquid essence of *Vespa mandarinia japonica*, it had been the beverage of choice of Naoko Takahashi on her way to her gold medal in the Olympic marathon at Sydney. Monica's father brings it home to his athlete wife and daughters from business trips to Tokyo. Monica's mother, Jane Wojcik, has run marathons in thirty-one of the fifty states, now and again after training on bee spit. In powder form, it comes out of a silvery packet and quickly dissolves in water. Characters covering the packets tell some of the bee-spit story. *Vespa mandarinia japonica*—the Japanese giant hornet—flies about a hundred kilometres a day ingesting but not digesting small insects, which it carries home in globular form to feed to its larvae. The juice that goes for the gold is in the larvae. While the adult feeds the larvae, the larvae reciprocate with fresh juice, a blend of seventeen amino acids. The acids rapidly burn the adult hornet's abdominal fat, releasing the energy on which the adult flies another hundred kilometres ingesting small insects. Vaam, vaam, thank you, ma'am—Vespa amino-acid mixture. If you are not into cycling or marathon runs, you can sit on a sofa, drink Vaam, and lose weight. Monica primed me with another glass of bee spit before another sixteen miles, a week or two later. To be honest, it failed to turn me into Barry Bonds. I cannot say that it was any more effective than the shot of bourbon I have every night before dinner. But it put a new entry at the top of my life list:

bee spit
burdock
caribou
catnip tea
cattail sprouts
chickweed
chicory
coachwhip
conch
Dall sheep
dandelions
deer
dock
durian
grizzly
ground-cherries
groundnuts
Jerusalem artichokes
lamb's-quarters
lion

MY LIFE LIST

mallow cheeses

moose

mountain oysters

musk ox

muskrat

ostrich

oyster mushrooms

pennyroyal tea

persimmons

porpoise

puffin

rattlesnake

sea cucumber

snapping-turtle eggs

water-mint tea

weasel

whale

white-pine-needle tea

wild mustard

wild-spearmint tea

winter cress

wintergreen berries

witch-hazel tea

CHECKPOINTS

$\int$ ara Lippincott, who now lives in Pasadena, having retired as an editor at *The New Yorker* in the early nineteen-nineties, worked in the magazine's fact-checking department from 1966 until 1982. She had a passion for science, and when pieces of writing about science came in to the magazine they were generally copied to her desk. In 1973, a long piece of mine called "The Curve of Binding Energy" received her full-time attention for three or four weeks and needed every minute of it. Explaining her work to an audience at a journalism school, Sara once said, "Each word in the piece that has even a shred of fact clinging to it is scrutinized, and, if passed, given the checker's imprimatur, which consists of a tiny pencil tick." From that sixty-thousand-word piece of mine—which was about weapons-grade nuclear material in private industry and what terrorists might or might not do with it—one paragraph in particular stands out in memory for the degree of difficulty it presented to her and the effort she made to keep it or kill it.

It was a story told to me by John A. Wheeler, who, during the Second World War, had been the leading physicist in residence at the Hanford Engineer Works, on the Columbia River in south-central Washington, where he attended the startup and plutonium production of the first large-scale nuclear reactor in the world. In 1939, with the Danish physicist Niels Bohr, Wheeler had identified the atomic nuclei most prone to fission and the consequent release of binding energy. In 1943–44, as the first reactor was being designed for Hanford, Wheeler had urged that its fundamental cross-section be expanded from a circle to a square, so that five hundred extra fuel rods could be inserted, if necessary, into the graphite matrix of the reactor—a colossally expensive alteration made because Wheeler had come to suspect that something like xenon poisoning might affect the reaction. It did, and the increased neutron flux from the additional fuel rods took care of the problem. In Professor Wheeler's office at Princeton University in 1973, I had scribbled notes for about an hour when he said, as a kind of afterthought, that an odd thing happened at Hanford in the winter of 1944–45, or, perhaps, did not happen. He had not observed it himself. He had never seen it mentioned in print. Hanford was a vast, spread-out place in the bunchgrass country, full of rumors, secrecy, and apocryphal stories. If I were to use this story, I would have to authenticate it on my own because he had no idea if it was true. He said he had heard that a Japanese incendiary balloon—one of the weapon balloons that were released in Japan and carried by the jet stream across the Pacific Ocean—had landed on the reactor that was making the plutonium that destroyed Nagasaki, and had shut the reactor down.

The Japanese called the balloons *fūsen bakudan*. Thirty-three feet in diameter, they were made of paper and were equipped with incendiary devices or high explosives. In less than a year, nine thousand were launched from a beach on Honshu. They killed six people in Oregon, five of them children, and they started forest fires, and they landed from Alaska to Mexico and as far east as Farmington, Michigan, a suburb of Detroit. Completing the original manuscript of "The Curve of Binding Energy," which was otherwise not about Hanford, I wrote half a dozen sentences on the balloon that shut down the reactor, and I turned the piece in. If Wheeler's story was true, it would make it into print. If unverifiable, it would be deleted. I hoped it was true. The rest was up to Sara.

Her telephone calls ricocheted all over the United States: from Brookhaven to Bethesda, from La Jolla to Los Alamos, not to mention Hanford and various targets in the District of Columbia. Interspersed with everything else she had to do in order to arrive—one word at a time—at those countless ticks, she went on making calls about the incendiary balloon for days on end. At last came an apparent breakthrough. Someone told her that he could not authenticate the story, but he knew absolutely who could.

"Oh, yes? Who?"

"John Wheeler."

I told Sara to abandon the anecdote. The tale was almost surely someone's invention; we should just delete it; she had done enough. She went on making phone calls.

If Sara was looking for information in the dark, the darkness was the long shadow of the wartime secrecy, when forty-five thousand people, from construction workers to theoreticians, lived in Hanford, Pasco, Kennewick, and, especially, Richland, a village of two hundred that the Army bought in 1943 and soon enhanced with more than four thousand houses. The large population notwithstanding, Hanford Engineer Works, of the Manhattan Project, was so secret that the Joint Chiefs of Staff did not know about it. Harry Truman learned of it only after the death of Franklin Roosevelt, in April, 1945. People at Hanford lived among posters that said "Don't Be Caught with Your Mouth Open." They set their urine in bottles on their doorsteps at night so it could be tested for contained plutonium. The people of Richland made babies at a higher rate than any other place in the nation. There was little else to make except plutonium. To put an ear to the ground, so to speak, and listen for spies, a resident F.B.I. agent went to brothels in Pasco and Kennewick, taking with him his beautiful wife. She sat in the car while he did his counterespionage inside. To profile people who might be easy targets for spies, F.B.I. agents went from house to house trying to learn who the heavier drinkers were and who was climbing into what neighbor's bed. Hanford Engineer Works had its own justices of the peace, its own jail. Taverns were erected for the nighttime bibulation of construction workers, whose tendency to brawl was so intense that Wheeler later recalled "those beer joints with windows close to ground level so that tear gas could be squirted in."

Key personnel were known by false names. Enrico Fermi was Mr. Farmer. Eugene Wigner was Mr. Winger. Arthur Compton was Mr. Comas. People referred to Wheeler as Johnny the Genie. Radiation exposure was called "shine," and the word for radiation itself was "activity." One technician who slipped up and used the "R" word was called to an office and chewed. With extremely few exceptions, the personnel had no idea what they were doing, but they did what they were told. ("We all washed our hands so many times a day I thought I was Lady Macbeth.") The Manhattan Project, at Hanford as elsewhere, required the " 'immediate high amputation' of any human limb with a cut contaminated by plutonium." There could have been a safety billboard: 29 DAYS WITHOUT A HUMERUS LOST. There were black-widow spiders in people's houses. One woman called the government hospital and asked what she should do if a black widow bit her three-year-old daughter. Hospital: "If she goes into convulsions, bring her in. . . ." On and off the site, rumors were ceaseless about Hanford's contribution to the war effort: variously, it was a P.O.W. camp, a processor of solid rocket fuel, a biological kitchen preparing things for germ warfare, a nylon production line (DuPont was the prime industrial contractor). Asked what was really going on, the Army's knowledgeable liaison, Captain Frank Valente, said, "We are dehydrating the Columbia River for shipment overseas."

And now, in late 1973 at *The New Yorker*, the moment was rapidly approaching when "The Curve of Binding Energy" would go to press and alterations would no longer be possible. Once again, I thanked Sara and told her to remove the story of the Japanese balloon. O.K., she said, but maybe if she found a free moment that final afternoon she would make another call or two. Or three. And she did, and she turned up someone in Delaware who told her that he could not authenticate the story, but he knew absolutely who could.

Oh? Who would that be? John Wheeler?

The site manager, B Reactor. He would surely have known if an incendiary balloon had lit up his building.

Where is he now?

Retired in Florida.

Sara looked up his telephone number. The checking department in those days was equipped floor to ceiling with telephone books. She called. He was not home. He had gone shopping.

Where?

The mall.

Sara called the police. She told them the situation, asked for help, and gave them her telephone number.

Minutes went by but not hours. The piece had not yet gone to press when the site manager called. He was in a telephone booth, the ancestral cell. Sara explained her purpose and read to him a passage that ended as follows:

> The fire balloons were so successful, in fact, that papers were asked not to print news of them, because the United States did not want to encourage the Japanese to release more. The balloon that reached Hanford crossed not only the Pacific but also the Olympic Mountains and the alpine glaciers of the Cascade Range. It now landed on the building containing the reactor that was producing the Nagasaki plutonium, and shut the reactor down.

The manager said to Sara, "How did you know that?"

He went on to say that the balloon had not actually landed on the building but on a high-tension line carrying power to the reactor. Striking the line, the balloon burst into flames.

There was just enough time to make the fix.

A-Rod makes an occasional error, and so does *The New Yorker*. Rarest of all is a fact that was not erroneous in the original manuscript but became an error in the checking process. When this happens, it can fairly be called an event, like the day the soap sank at Procter & Gamble. This has happened to me only once—and nearly thirty years ago. If blame is to be assigned, heaven forbid, I am not the assignee, and neither is Sara, who checked the piece. Called "Basin and Range," it was the first in a series of long pieces on geology that appeared from time to time across a dozen years. It had extensive introductory passages on themes like plate tectonics and geologic time. In the original manuscript, one paragraph said:

> It is the plates that move. They all move. They move in varying directions and at different speeds. The Adriatic Plate is moving north. The African Plate once came up behind it and drove it into Europe—drove Italy like a nail into Europe—and thus created the Alps.

C Issue, B Issue, A Issue, the schedule drifted, as ever, toward the brink of time, the final and irreversible closing. In one's head as in the surrounding building, things speed up in the ultimate hours and can become, to say the least, frenetic. Joshua Hersh, a modern fact-checker who is characteristically calmer than marble, refers to this zone of time as "the last-minute heebie-jeebies." As "Basin and Range" came within fifteen minutes of closing, so many rocks were flying around in my head that I would have believed Sara if she had told me that limestone is the pit of a fruit. At one minute to zero, she came to tell me that I was wrong about the Adriatic Plate, that it is not moving north but southwest.

Desperately, I said, "Who told you that?"

She said, "Eldridge Moores."

World-class plate theorist, author of innumerable scientific papers on the ophiolitic sequence as the signature of global tectonics, president to be of the Geological Society of America, Eldridge Moores was the generous and quixotic geologist who had undertaken to teach me, on field trip after field trip, the geologic history of, among other places, California, Arizona, Greece, and Cyprus. My head spinning, I said to Sara, "If Eldridge Moores says the Adriatic Plate is moving southwest, it's moving southwest. Please change the sentence."

In the new *New Yorker* on the following Monday, the Adriatic Plate was on its way to Morocco. Leafing through the magazine in an idle moment that week, I called Eldridge and found him in his office at the University of California, Davis. I said, "Eldridge, if the Adriatic Plate is moving southwest, what are the Alps doing there?"

He said, "The Adriatic Plate?"

I said, "The Adriatic Plate."

I believe I actually heard him slap his forehead. "Oh, no!" he said. "Not the Adriatic Plate! The Aegean Plate. The Aegean Plate is moving southwest."

The worst checking error is calling people dead who are not dead. In the words of Josh Hersh, "It really annoys them." Sara remembers a reader in a nursing home who read in *The New Yorker* that he was "the late" reader in the nursing home. He wrote demanding a correction. *The New Yorker*, in its next issue, of course complied, inadvertently doubling the error, because the reader died over the weekend while the magazine was being printed.

Any error is everlasting. As Sara told the journalism students, once an error gets into print it "will live on and on in libraries carefully catalogued, scrupulously indexed . . . silicon-chipped, deceiving researcher after researcher down through the ages, all of whom will make new errors on the strength of the original errors, and so on and on into an exponential explosion of errata."

With drawn sword, the fact-checker stands at the near end of this bridge. It is, in part, why the job exists and why, in Sara's words, a publication will believe in "turning a pack of professional skeptics loose on its own galley proofs." Newspapers do not have discrete fact-checking departments, but many magazines do. When I first worked at *Time*—in the year 957, during the reign of Eadwig the All-Fair—*Time*'s writers were men, and the researcher/fact-checkers were women. They were expert. When I freelanced a piece to *The Atlantic*, I asked who would do the fact-checking and was told, "That's up to you." *The Atlantic* had a nil budget for fact-checking. A little later, when I sold a piece to *National Geographic* it seemed to have more fact-checkers than there are Indians in the Amazon. *Holiday* and the *Saturday Evening Post* were only a little less assiduous. While *The New Yorker*'s fact-checking department had achieved early fame in its field, many other magazines have been just as committed and careful. Twenty-eight years after that first *Atlantic* piece, I sold *The Atlantic* a second one, and this time experienced a checking process equivalent to *The New Yorker*'s.

Book publishers prefer to regard fact-checking as the responsibility of authors, which, contractually, comes down to a simple matter of who doesn't pay for what. If material that has appeared in a fact-checked magazine reappears in a book, the author is not the only beneficiary of the checker's work. The book publisher has won a free ticket to factual respectability. Publishers who, for early-marketing purposes, set a text in stone before a magazine's checking department has been through it get what they deserve. An almost foolproof backup screen to the magazine-to-book progression is the magazine's vigilant readership. After an error gets into *The New Yorker*, heat-seeking missiles rise off the earth and home in on the author, the fact-checker, the editor, and even the shade of the founder. As the checking department summarizes it, "No mistakes go unnoticed by readers." In the waning days of 2005, Rebecca Curtis's fine short story "Twenty Grand" appeared in *The New Yorker*. Its characters, in 1979, go into a McDonald's for Chicken McNuggets. McNuggets appeared in *The New Yorker*'s Christmas mail. McDonald's had introduced them nationwide in 1983.

On the scattered occasions when such a message has come to me, I have written to the reader a note of thanks (unless the letter is somewhere on the continuum between mean-spirited and nasty, which is rarely the case). "You're right!" I say. "And I am very grateful to you, because that mistake will not be present when the piece appears in book form." If, in the reader's letter, there has been just a tonal hint of a smirk, I cannot help adding, "If a lynx-eyed reader like you has gone through those thousands of words and has found only one mistake, I am quite relieved."

If there is one collection of people even more likely than *New Yorker* readers to notice mistakes of any ilk or origin, it is the Swiss. Around the first of October, 1983, Richard Sacks, a fact-checking veteran with oak-leaf clusters, put on his headphones and dialed Zurich. In weeks that followed, he also called Bern, Brig, Lausanne, Geneva, Salgesch, Sion, Sierre, and other communities, many of them in the Canton de Vaud, principal home of the Swiss Army's Tenth Mountain Division, which had given me a woolly hat and allowed me to walk around in the Bernese Oberland and the Pennine Alps with the Section de Renseignements of the Eighth Battalion, Fifth Regiment. Eventually, I wrote:

> With notebooks and pencils, the patrols of the Section de Renseignements go from place to place exploring, asking questions, collecting particulars, scribbling information, characterizing and describing people and scenes, doing reconnaissance of various terrains, doing surveillance of present activity, and tracking events of the recent past. Afterward, they trudge back and, under pressure of time, compress, arrange, and present what they have heard and seen. All of that is incorporated into the substance of the word "renseignements." I have limitless empathy for the Section de Renseignements.

No problem there. All Richard had to do was ask, phrase by phrase, if the patrols did those things. If he had to ask in French, he also asked for someone who could speak English, the better to tick the phrases. There were, however, extended dimensions of the situation.

> Generally speaking, it can be said that discipline is nearly perfect in the Swiss Army, and that discipline is perhaps a little less than perfect if the soldiers are thinking in French, and, finally, that within any French-speaking battalion perfection tends to dilapidate in the Section de Renseignements.

How would you put that in a call to an official in the Département Militaire? I had made very formal application to attend a so-called refresher course (a cours de répétition) with units of the national militia, and had included only one stipulation: that I spend at least fifty per cent of my time not in the company of officers. Evidently, the Département Militaire had no difficulty deciding where to place me.

According to majors and manuals, Renseignements is an activity that calls for a special style of mind, constantly seeking intelligence and finding it even if it is not there, for in peacetime exercises what is required above all else is imagination. The effect of the Section de Renseignements is, in one major's words, "to make it live."

That is to say, people in Renseignements need a fact-checker.

The patrols of Renseignements walk in the unoccupied territory between the battalion and the enemy. They circle high behind enemy lines. Since the mountains are real and the enemy is not, there tends to be a certain diminution of energy during a refresher course—particularly on the part of those who go out on patrol, in contrast to those who stay in the command post and think up things for the patrols to do. Essentially, the people in the command posts are editors, trying to make sense of the information presented by the patrols, and by and large the patrols are collections of miscellaneous freelancing loners, who lack enthusiasm for the military enterprise, have various levels of antipathy to figures of authority, and, in a phrase employed by themselves and their officers alike, are "the black sheep of the army."

I would admire the Swiss forever for having the wit to assign me to Renseignements—a legerdemain of public relations unheard of in my country. Our patrol was led by a young viticul-teur named Luc Massy, whose love of Switzerland was in inverse proportion to his love for the Army. He carried on patrol his assault rifle, his tire-bouchon, and his six-centilitre verre de cave. The several wines concealed in his pack bulged like a cord of mortar shells. In an alpine meadow, the patrol sits down in a circle.

Massy fills the glass, holds it up to his eye. "Santé," he says, with a nod to the rest of us, and—thoughtfully, unhurriedly—drinks it himself. Because I happen to be sitting beside him on his left, he says, "John, you are not very well placed. In my town, we drink counterclockwise." After finishing the glass, he fills it again and hands it to his right—to Jean Reidenbach. The background music is a dissonance of cattle bells. We count nineteen Brown Swiss in the meadow just below us, and they sound like the Sal-vation Army. A narrow red train appears far below. Coming out of a tunnel it crosses a bridge, whistling—three cars in all, the Furka-Oberalp.

In his weeks on the telephone with Switzerland, Richard Sacks had a great deal more to do than retrace the steps of one patrol from alp to alp, or call an off-limits restaurant in Birgisch where Corporal Massy stirred fondue with the antenna of a walkie-talkie. There remained that other half of the equation, the officers: the major who managed the Hotel zum Storchen, in Zurich; the colonel who was also president of Credit Suisse; the major who was general manager of the Bankverein; the colonel who was president of the Bankgesellschaft; the colonel who was chairman of Hoffmann-La Roche; the major who was chairman of Ciba-Geigy; the major who imported lobsters from Maine and had been caught entering Sweden with bundles of cash taped to his legs. Richard could not get a hard check on that last one, and we left it out of the piece. Captain François Rumpf was my official shepherd and initial contact. A letter from the Département Militaire instructed me after arriving in Switzerland to meet him on a precise day and hour in the Second Class Buffet in the railway station of Lausanne. I was there, on the Swiss dot. Rumpf was adjutant to Adrien Tschumy, the tall, contemplative Divisionnaire—two stars and a full-time professional. He reported to Enrico Franchini, of Canton Ticino, Commandant de Corps.

> He had a kindly face that was somewhat wrinkled and drawn. There were three stars on his cap, and down the sides of his legs ran the broad black stripes of the general staff, disappearing into low black boots. Sometimes described as "mysterious" and "not well known outside Ticino," he was one of the seven supreme commanders of the Swiss Army.

I had worked through the final draft of the manuscript during a month at an academic retreat in northern Italy, where I had little else to do but show up for cocktails at five in the evening. I have never turned in to *The New Yorker* a more combed-over piece than that one. Its length was around forty thousand words. As Richard went through them a tick at a time—starting on the telephone in the early morning and staying on the telephone until the end of the Swiss day—he found, as he always did, errors resulting from words misheard, errors of assumption and supposition, errors of misinformation from flawed books or living sources, items misinterpreted or misunderstood. To turn up that many errors in so long a piece was routine in his work, and scarcely a surprise to me. I both expected it and depended on it in the way that I have relied on the colleagueship of professional fact-checkers for fifty years. In the making of a long piece of factual writing, errors will occur, and in ways invisible to the writer. Was the Morgenstern really an eight-foot cudgel with a sixteen-spike pineapple head? Is the Schwarzbergalp above the Mattmarksee? Would you get to the Nussbaum bridge via Gouchheit, Krizacher, and Vogelture? Would the villages be in that order? Are there two h's in Gouchheit? How many n's in Othmar Hermann Ammann? How long would it take an entire company to go up the Bettmeralp téléphérique? How many soldiers could sleep in the Schwarzenbach barn? Was that all right with Schwarzenbach? What is the correct spelling of Schweizerische Bankgesellschaft? Of Schweizerische Kreditanstalt? Of Schweizerischer Bankverein? Who wrote the cuckoo-clock speech in Graham Greene's "The Third Man"? Did Louis Chevrolet, of Canton de Neuchâtel, really put the map of Switzerland on the grilles of his American cars? Richard called Warren, Michigan.

Richard to me, as he remembers it: "Chevy says no. Chevy denies it."

Me: "Not everything that Chevy says is right." The Musée des Suisses à l'Étranger, near Geneva, says that a map is what Chevrolet had in mind, that his emblem "n'est pas sans rappeler, de façon stylisée, le pays d'origine du constructeur."

In "The Third Man," in the immortal Ferris-wheel scene high above postwar Vienna, Orson Welles as Harry Lime implies that he has been selling diluted penicillin to Viennese hospitals but asks his lifelong friend Joseph Cotten if one of those little moving dots down there (one of those human beings) could really matter in the long scheme of things. On the ground, he adds:

> In Italy for thirty years under the Borgias, they had warfare, terror, murder, bloodshed—but they produced Michelangelo, Leonardo da Vinci, and the Renaissance. In Switzerland, they had brotherly love, five hundred years of democracy and peace, and what did that produce? The cuckoo clock.

I learned, or Richard learned—we've forgotten who learned—that Graham Greene, who wrote the screenplay of "The Third Man," only later published the preliminary treatment as a novella, and the cuckoo-clock speech does not appear either in the novella or in the original screenplay. Greene did not write it. Orson Welles thought it up and said it.

After the Swiss Army piece appeared in *The New Yorker*, I expected a swarm of letters containing nits that only a Swiss could pick. Those *New Yorker* issues (October 31 and November 7, 1983) were read in Switzerland more widely than I ever would have guessed. Some months later, the book that reprinted them sold well there, too, actually reaching very high on the national list, the fact notwithstanding that the book was in English. Yet as a result of Richard's fact-checking no word has ever come to me from Switzerland (or, for that matter, from anywhere else) of an error in the English version. The French version was done by two translators for a publisher in Paris. A hundred and forty errors were found in it by the adjutant François Rumpf, who fixed them himself for a second printing.

Richard Sacks moved on from *The New Yorker* to *The Reader's Digest* and has retired from the *Digest* to the lone preoccupations of a novelist. I said to him recently how impressed I continue to be that in more than a quarter of a century no Swiss has sent a corrective letter about that story.

This fact did not check out with Richard. "Oh, but there was one letter," he said. "Something about a German word, but the reader was wrong."

In a 1993 essay on Sylvia Plath and Ted Hughes and the three decades of biographies that had described them, Janet Malcolm mentioned a plaque on the house in London where Plath was living with her two children when she died. The galley proof said:

> Olwyn and I finally reached the house on Fitzroy Road where Plath killed herself. I recognized it immediately—it is an obligatory photographic subject of the Plath biographies, and its oval blue ceramic plaque reading "William Butler Yeats, 1865–1939, Irish poet and dramatist, lived here" is a compulsively mentioned (and yet oddly irrelevant) detail.

"Irrelevant" is not a word that travels far in the checking department. The checker called *The New Yorker*'s London office, a species of exaggeration where three and sometimes four people worked on an upper floor in an old building in Hay Hill, Mayfair. One was a young English cyclist named Matt Seaton, whose title was London Bureau Manager. Now a columnist for the *Guardian*, Seaton vividly remembers the call about the plaque: "The checker was very specific in requesting that I actually go see it to ascertain that it was indeed blue and ceramic (as opposed to, say, black enamel tin) . . . I found the errand slightly absurd/ amusing, because if you live in London you know there are plaques like this all over, and they're all basically the same." Seaton nevertheless descended the stairs, got on his bicycle, and went via Portland Place to the outer circle road around Regent's Park and then up Primrose Hill to 23 Fitzroy to check the Yeats plaque.

In the nineteen-eighties, Michelle Preston checked a piece on the iconography of New York City street signs. She went out and looked at the signs and "just about all of them were wrong." The signs weren't wrong; the writer was; and the piece was O.K. because the facts could be professionally corrected. Less easily realigned was a checking proof in which the writer bushwhacked uphill through wild terrain to a certain summit in the Appalachians. The checker went to the mountain and found that she could drive to the top. If a writer writes that Santa Claus went down a chimney wearing a green suit, the color will be challenged, and the checker will try to learn Santa's waist measurement and the chimney's interior dimensions. Not only is fiction checked but also cartoon captions and the drawings themselves. When two cars passing an American gas station were each driving on the left side of the road, a checker noticed. The image had been flipped in reproduction.

Humor is checked in all forms, sometimes causing fact-checkers to be cast as obtuse. Joshua Hersh is not fond of this hair shirt. "We understand humor; we are real people," he asserts. "But we have to ask: 'Do you mean this humorously? Is that a joke or a mistake?'"

It could be both. In a piece called "Farewell to the Nineteenth Century"—which described the Kennebec River now, then, and earlier—I mentioned that the schooner Hesperus was built in Hallowell, Maine, downstream of Augusta. I said that the Hesperus had been "wrecked multiguously by Henry Wadsworth Longfellow." The fact-checker looked into it. Then—in a tone that was a wee bit stern and adversarial, not to mention critical—she said to me: "Longfellow did not wreck the Hesperus!"

I was surprised to be told by Richard Sacks recently that *The New Yorker* once checked people's anecdotes and claims and so forth only with the source, and not—or not as a rule, anyway—with third parties. If someone said he was Jerome Kern's cousin, he was Jerome Kern's cousin, tick, tick, tick. The fact-checkers certainly triangulate now. If three sources tell the same story, there is a reasonable probability that under enough additional inquiry it may be thought correct. I once heard Brock Brower say of the research process for non-fiction writing that you have probably done enough "when you meet yourself coming the other way." Fact-checking is like that, too, of course. Today's fact-checkers always start with the Internet, they tell me, and then ramify through the New York Public Library and beyond—a pilgrimage from the errant to the trustworthy. In the nineteen-sixties, acting within some legislated legalese known as "the mining exception," Kennecott Copper planned an open pit in the Glacier Peak Wilderness of the North Cascades. The Sierra Club said the mine would be visible from the moon. With the additional counsel of planetary scientists, the checking department decided that it would not be.

When the novelist Susan Diamond was a fact-checker at *The New Yorker* she called a number in San Francisco one day, and said, "Is this the city water department?"

Voice on phone: "No. This is Acme Air Conditioning."

Susan: [*pause*] "Well, perhaps you can help me."

Overhearing bits of conversation was not a feat. The departmental space at 25 West Forty-third Street, where *The New Yorker* spent the fifty-six years ending in 1991, was basically one room in which seven desks were tightly packed among piled books and tumbling paper. Easily traversable in five steps, it closely resembled the communications center in George Washington's headquarters at Valley Forge, where twenty officers in a twelve-by-twelve-foot room sat all day long writing letters. Sara remembers a German fact-checker named Helga, who was "spiffy-looking, with long hair." When Kennedy Fraser wrote a piece on a furniture store, calling its furniture "ersatz," Helga called the store. "Tell me," she said. "Do you have any ersatz furniture?" Dusty Mortimer-Maddox, a great checker who held the job for almost as many years as Martin Baron, at one point had a fur-covered telephone. In the room on Forty-third Street, a cruciform emblem said "God Bless Our Home." After Jewish checkers objected, the cross was put on the department's reference Bible. When the magazine crossed the street, in 1991, the cross crossed with it. When the magazine moved to Times Square, in 1999, the cross went to the Crossroads of the World. Twice as many checkers now work in three times as much space as the department had at 25 West Forty-third Street. Martin Baron has been through every scene described. He is a fact-checker so learned in the procedures of scholarship that an editor once said to me, "Always remember this about Martin: he is never wrong." This was not a character judgment. It was just a checkable fact. Martin was checking a story by Ken Auletta on the day that Auletta married the literary agent Amanda "Binky" Urban. Shortly before the ceremony, Martin was in Ken and Binky's apartment, with galley proofs, checking facts with the groom.

And more facts. The bride was on the roof, sunbathing. When she came down, she said, "Martin, I love you, but you have to go now because we have to get married."

Robert Bingham, gone since 1982, was an author's editor of the highest rank and Executive Editor of the magazine. With Sara Lippincott, he devised a checker test. Sara described it, in part, when she spoke to the aspiring journalists: "What we want are people who . . . already know that there are nine men in a batting order, what a Republican is, and that the Earth is the third planet from the sun. That being got past, it helps if you speak French, German, Spanish, Italian, and Russian, read classical Greek, have low blood pressure, love your fellow man, and don't have to leave town on weekends." The checker test was a great deal more challenging than the examples Sara gives. It was the sort of thing Republican presidents routinely flunk. Who is the Sultan of Oman? Who is the Emir of Qatar? Who is the King of Bhutan? Who is the Secretary of Health and Human Services? What is acetylsalicylic acid? Last night, where was the Dow? (That last one was Bingham's way of assessing poets.) Over time, as new candidates came along, the test was updated and modified. When Michelle Preston came along, in the nineteen-eighties, she achieved the checker test's highest all-time score. Like her husband, Richard Preston, she is now among *The New Yorker*'s contributors.

In the comfortable knowledge that the fact-checking department is going to follow up behind me, I like to guess at certain names and numbers early on, while I change and re-change and listen to sentences, preferring to hear some ballpark figure or approximate date than the dissonant clink of journalistic terms: WHAT CITY,

$000,000, name TK, number TK, Koming. These are forms of promissory note, and a checker is expected to pay it. Koming means what koming sounds like and is sort of kute; TK means "to come." At least for me, they don't serve the sound of a drafted sentence as well as flat-out substitutes, pro-tem inventions. In a freight train a mile and a half long, there is a vital tube of air that runs the full length and controls the brakes. In "Coal Train" (2005), I felt a need for analogy and guessed at one:

> The releasing of the air brakes began at the two ends, and moved toward the middle. The train's very long integral air tube was like the air sac of an American eel.

Before long, the checking department was up to its chin in ichthyologists, and I was informed by Josh Hersh that the air sac of an American eel is proportionally a good deal shorter than the air sac in most ordinary fish.

"Who says so?"

"Willy Bemis."

"Oh."

Willy Bemis is to the anatomy of fishes what Eldridge Moores is to tectonics. Willy was the central figure in a book of mine that had been published three years before, parts of which appeared in *The New Yorker*. He had since left the University of Massachusetts to become director of Shoals Marine Laboratory, the offshore classrooms of Cornell University and the University of New Hampshire. I called him in Ithaca to ask what could be done. Ever accommodating, Willy at first tried to rationalize the eel. Maybe its air sac was up to the job after all. Maybe the analogy would work. I said the eel would never make it through the checking department, or, for that matter, past me. We were close to closing, and right offhand Willy was unable to think of a species with a long enough sac. What to do? What else? He called Harvard. The train's very long integral air tube was like the air sac of a rope fish.

On the Merrimack River in Merrimack, New Hampshire, is a Budweiser brewery that brewed its first Bud in 1970. In 1839, John and Henry Thoreau passed the site in their homemade skiff on the journey that resulted in Henry's first book. A run of white water there had been known as Cromwell's Falls since the seventeenth century, but, Thoreau wrote, "these falls are the Nesenkeag of the Indians," and he went on to say, "Great Nesenkeag Stream comes in on the right just above." New Hampshire has a number of place names that end in the letters "k e a g." The "keag" is pronounced as if the "a" were missing, i.e., "keg." In 2003, my son-in-law Mark Svenvold and I went through Nesenkeag Falls and Namaskeag Falls and Amoskeag Falls, in an Old Town canoe, tracing the Thoreaus' upstream journey, and while dragging the canoe up the rapids I found myself wondering how many kegs that Budweiser plant could produce in a day. Back home and writing, I made up a number out of thin air, and it is what Anne Stringfield, checking the facts, saw on her proof:

> Just above Cromwell's Falls on Route 3, very close to but not visible from the river, is a Budweiser brewery that has a production average of thirteen thousand kegs a day.

Never underestimate Anheuser-Busch. The average production turned out to be eighteen thousand kegs a day.

Another fluvial piece—"Tight-Assed River"—was checked by Josh Hersh in 2004. He found this on his proof:

> People say, "The Illinois River? What's that? Never heard of it. Where does it go?" Actually, there are two Illinois Rivers in America, each, evidently, as well known as the other.

One is in Illinois, another is in Arkansas and Oklahoma; and those two are all you will find in Merriam-Webster's Geographical Dictionary, which is among the checking department's more revered references. Josh dove into the Web, and came up with a third—an Illinois River in Oregon, which is not well known even in Oregon.

> Actually, there are three Illinois Rivers in America, each, evidently, as well known as the others.

(Checking this piece before it appeared in *The New Yorker* in February 2009, the fact-checking department found yet another Illinois River—in Colorado. If I were to republish this bit of fluvial information forty-six more times, evidently we would find an Illinois River in every state in the Union.) That feat, on Josh's part, was just a stretching exercise before he took on, among other things, a cabin boat that was drifting idly on the eponymous Illinois while a vessel longer than an aircraft carrier bore down upon it sounding five short blasts, the universal statement of immediate danger. The vessel, more than eleven hundred feet long and wired rigid, was made up of fifteen barges pushed by a "towboat." I was in the pilothouse scribbling notes.

At just about the point where the cabin boat would go into our blind spot—the thousand feet of water that we in the pilothouse can't see—people appear on the cabin boat's deck, the boat starts up, and in a manner that seems both haughty and defiant moves slowly and slightly aside. We grind on downriver as the boat moves up to pass us port to port, making its way up the thousand feet of barges to draw even with the pilothouse. Two men and two women are in the cabin boat. The nearest woman— seated left rear in the open part of the cockpit—is wearing a black-and-gold two-piece bathing suit. She has the sort of body you go to see in marble. She has golden hair. Quickly, deftly, she reaches with both hands behind her back and unclasps her top. Setting it on her lap, she swivels ninety degrees to face the towboat square. Shoulders back, cheeks high, she holds her pose without retreat. In her ample presentation there is defiance of gravity. There is no angle of repose. She is a siren, and these are her songs.

So far so checkable. Something like that can be put "on author." It was my experience, my description, my construction, my erection. No one seemed worried about the color of the bathing suit. I went on, though, to say something close to this:

She is Henry Moore's "Oval with Points." Moore said, "Rounded forms convey an idea of fruitfulness, maturity, probably because the earth, women's breasts, and most fruits are rounded, and these shapes are important because they have this background in our habits of perception. I think the humanist organic element will always be for me of fundamental importance in sculpture."

And now we were into deep checking. In 1975, I had telephoned Lynn Fraker, who was a docent for the art museum at Princeton, where Moore's "Oval with Points" is one of a couple of dozen very large and primarily abstract sculptures that stand outdoors around the campus. I wanted to use them as description exercises in a writing class that I was about to teach for the first time. The Henry Moore, eleven feet tall, is shaped like a doughnut, and from each of its interior sides a conical and breastlike bulge extends toward another conical and breastlike bulge, their business ends nearly touching, as if they were on the ceiling of a chapel. It was my opinion that students should be able to do a better description than that. "Doughnut," for example, was not a word that should be allowed to rise into the company of Henry Moore, and, in every class I have taught since then, I have used the notes from that talk with Lynn Fraker. They include the words of Henry Moore, which she recited from memory. And now in 2004 I had no idea where she read them. She had left Princeton decades before, had remarried, and was at that time unreachable.

The Internet was no help, but Josh, searching through the catalogues of the New York Public Library, learned that collections of Moore's commentaries on sculptural art were in a midtown branch, across Fifth Avenue from the library's main building. After an hour or two there, he found an essay by Moore from a 1937 issue of the BBC's *The Listener*. In the next-to-last paragraph were the words that Lynn Fraker had rattled off to me.

They needed very little adjustment to be rendered verbatim, as they are above. After which, we were back to "on author":

> She has not moved—this half-naked Maja outnakeding the whole one. Her nipples are a pair of eyes staring the towboat down. For my part, I want to leap off the tow, swim to her, and ask if there is anything I can do to help.

Perhaps I am giving the fact-checkers too much credit. After all, I do what they do before they do. I don't leave a mountain of work to them, and this is especially true if *The New Yorker* has rejected the piece and I am forging ahead to include it in a book, as happened in 2002, when the magazine turned a cold eye—for some inexplicable reason—on twelve thousand words about the American history of a fish. So I checked the virginal parts of the book myself, risking analogy with the lawyer who defends himself and has a fool for a client. The task took me three months—trying to retrace the facts in the manuscript by as many alternate routes as I could think of, as fact-checkers routinely do. There were a couple of passages that slowed things down almost to a halt, when, for one reason or another, it took eons on the Internet and more time in libraries to determine what to do or not to do.

> Penn's daughter Margaret fished in the Delaware, and wrote home to a brother asking him to "buy for me a four joynted strong fishing Rod and Real with strong good Lines . . ."

The problem was not with the rod or the real but with William Penn's offspring. Should there be commas around Margaret or no commas around Margaret? The presence or absence of commas would, in effect, say whether Penn had one daughter or more than one. The commas—there or missing there—were not just commas; they were facts, neither more nor less factual than the kegs of Bud or the color of Santa's suit. Margaret, one of Penn's several daughters, went into the book without commas. Moving on, I tried to check this one:

On Wednesday, August 15, 1716, near Cambridge, Massachusetts, Cotton Mather fell out of a canoe while fishing on Spy Pond. After emerging soaked, perplexed, fishless, he said, "My God, help me to understand the meaning of it!" Before long, he was chastising his fellow clerics for wasting God's time in recreational fishing. Not a lot of warmth there. Better to turn to the clergyman Fluviatulis Piscator, known to his family as Joseph Seccombe, who was twenty-one years old when Cotton Mather died. Beside the Merrimack River, in 1739, Piscator delivered a sermon that was later published as "A Discourse utter'd in Part at Ammauskeeg-Falls, in the Fishing Season." There are nine copies in existence. One was sold at auction in 1986 for fourteen thousand dollars. The one I saw was at the Library Company of Philadelphia. Inserted in it was a book dealer's description that said, "First American book on angling; first American publication on sports of field and stream. Seccombe's defense of fishing is remarkable for coming so early, in a time when fishing for fun needed defending."

There was, in all of that, one part of one sentence that proved, in 2002, exceptionally hard to check. It could easily have been rewritten in a different way, but I stubbornly wished to check it. To wit:

Joseph Seccombe, who was twenty-one years old when Cotton Mather died.

In order to tick those exact and unmodified words, you would need to know not only the year in which Mather died and the year in which Seccombe was born but also the month and day for each. When Mather died, on February 13, 1728, Seccombe was either twenty-one or twenty-two. Which? The Internet failed me. Libraries failed me. The complete works of Joseph Seccombe and Fluviatulis Piscator failed me. I called Kingston, New Hampshire, where he had served as minister for more than twenty years. The person I reached generously said she would look through town and church records and call me back, which she did, two or three days later. She was sorry. She had looked long and hard, but in Kingston evidently the exact date of Seccombe's birth was nowhere to be found. I was about to give up and insert "in his early twenties" when a crimson lightbulb lit up in my head. If Joseph Seccombe was a minister in 1737 (the year he arrived in Kingston), he had been educated somewhere, and in those days in advanced education in the Province of Massachusetts Bay there was one game in town. I called Harvard.

By the main switchboard, I was put through to someone who listened to my question and said right back, within a few seconds, "June 14, 1706."

RIP VAN GOLFER

For many years, I have had a recurrent dream in which Lew Weiland's headlights, in the dark of night, appear like dawn above the tenth fairway. I am standing in a hazard that is really just a pond, and have been looking for balls. Against the dark bottom in the dark water, they glow like moons. There is muck between my toes and muck around my ankles, and I cannot easily move. Neither can Mike Hettinger or John Graham. We are caddies. Weiland is the greenskeeper. It is his custom and assumed priority to drain the pond from time to time, gather the lost balls, and split profits with the club pro, who sells them to the members. Golf balls have been a great scarcity since Pearl Harbor. The aurora over the tenth fairway grows ever brighter as Weiland races up rising ground, comes over a ridge, and floods us, stuck there, with direct light.

Caddies could play the course in the evening, and we did so into deep dusk. Aged thirteen, fourteen, I loved playing golf, even after carrying the big leather bags of lumber dealers, financiers, insurance salesmen, and osteopaths—going "doubles eighteen"—in the high humidity of a New Jersey summer. We were paid a dollar a bag, and tipped, if at all, in copper. No carts. I caddied only sporadically, when I needed money for a basketball or a baseball mitt. I caddied in Wisconsin one summer, and went to the Tam O'Shanter tournament in Chicago (Bobby Locke, the knickered South African; Jimmy Demaret, at 290 yards one of the longest balls in golf). And in 1950 I was beside the ropeless fairways glimpsing Ben Hogan in the Open at Merion. Soon, though, a day of epiphany came, on a specific round, when, aged twenty-four, clearly, if not for the first time, I envisioned golf as a psychological Sing Sing in which I was an inmate. Still young enough to effect an escape, I picked up the ball I was playing— Dunlop Maxfli 2—and put it in my pocket. I quit cold, not only as a player but also as an on-site spectator, and have not been on a golf course with a club in my hand since that day.

Yet now, after a fast-forwarding dormancy of more than fifty years, I am inside the ropes and close beside a back-nine tee, watching Tiger Woods making arcs in the air as he prepares his next shot in the 2007 U.S. Open. The ball is on its tee. A couple of yards toward the back of the tee box, Woods stands motionless, feet together, his gaze levelled on the fairway, his posture as per-pendicular as military attention. He steps forward and addresses the ball. About to hit, he hears the long whistle of a locomotive, on a track quite nearby. Approaching a grade crossing, the train completes its trombone chords: long, long, short, long. Woods backs off, waits. Now he re-addresses the ball. But another grade crossing is close to the first one. The engineer, at his console, again depresses his mushroom plunger. Woods again backs off, idly swings his club, resumes his pre-shot routine. Now, reorgan-ized, he is over the ball, but once again the engineer depresses the plunger. Backing off, Woods looks up at the sky. If only that engi-neer could know what he is interrupting, and whom, he would go away with a lifetime memento. The four-chord signal has become a little softer; and Woods is more than a little impatient. After two longs, he drills the ball on the short.

While the train was passing and whistling, it overrode the sound of the Pennsylvania Turnpike, which now, like breaking surf, returns. Seven holes are east of the turnpike, and eleven holes are west of the turnpike. Railroad track is close beside the highway. It could be said that no hazard on any golf course comes anywhere near rivalling these two, but in fact they are to a remarkable extent not only out of play but out of sight. Like a wide-open V, the topography of this great golf course in Oakmont, Pennsylvania, the first ever listed as a National Historic Landmark, descends from the clubhouse to the turnpike and then rises on the other side, as if the road were a river. Yet the right-of-way is so deeply incised that the road and the railroad are invisible, except when you are crossing them on one of the long, vertiginous footbridges that connect the first green to the second tee and the eighth green to the ninth tee.

No golfer present is going to finish this tournament under par, a fact that will not be unpleasing to the United States Golf Association, which chooses the annual venues and controls every aspect of the tournament, inside and outside the ropes. The U.S.G.A.'s annual intention is to make the U.S. Open globally the most difficult test in golf. By the players' clear consensus, that is what it is. The U.S.G.A. has chosen Oakmont, which is fourteen miles from Pittsburgh, eight times in eighty years. Why? Its credentials seem counterintuitive. It was laid out by a complete amateur at golf-course architecture—a fin-de-siècle iron-and-steel baron named Henry Clay Fownes, who, in his lifetime, designed one course, after Andrew Carnegie introduced him to the game.

In the words of Rand Jerris, the U.S.G.A.'s chief archivist, "Fownes wanted to make the hardest course in America. He did. A hundred years later, and only a few yards longer, it still is the hardest course in America."

Fairways are exceptionally narrow. Beside them, balls disappear even in primary rough. After the secondary, the grass is so high that it could be mown and sold as hay. Where drainage ditches hug some fairways, the rough is kept short between fairway and ditch so that errant balls can find the ditch. Most golf courses have about seventy bunkers. Oakmont has two hundred and ten. Balls become fried eggs in the soft quartz sand. One bunker, between parallel fairways and ribbed with grass benches, is 100 yards long. Seventeen is a short par 4, a dogleg with a drivable green. If you try driving it, you have to carry six bunkers at the dogleg and avoid five more bunkers penannular to the green. The largest one beside the green is Big Mouth. If you go into it, you can't see out. Big Mouth is eleven feet deep.

Oakmont has the longest par 3 (more than 300 yards if the pin is back) and the longest par 5 (nearly 700 yards) in the history of the U.S. Open, but those lengths—like the bunkers and the roughs and the astringent fairways—are modest challenges to these golfers relative to the vitreous greens. A slow six-foot putt misses, and goes thirty feet past the hole. A bunker shot lands ten feet above the hole, rolls, turns left, rolls back past the hole, and ends up twenty-five feet below it. Television pictures tend to flatten golf greens. You don't see on television the actual character of the putting surfaces—how warped they may be, how legible. Aaron Baddeley, an Australian born in the United States, magically sinks a ten-foot putt that exactly replicates the letter "U." Paul Casey, who is English, gets a media interview after Round 2, celebrating his eccentric score of 66. Under winds and in hot sun, the greens are becoming ever firmer and faster, he says. "The greens are going to get blue. This is the toughest golf course I've ever played. It's brutal."

What will the other players make of his great score?

"They probably will think I walked off after fourteen."

Oakmont greens are not covered with bent grass, as greens are on most Eastern courses. Oakmont uses a *Poa annua* of its own creation which bears few seeds and therefore results in what golfers describe as a "less pebbly" surface. No doubt about that. Ball after ball hits the greens, releases, and rolls to kingdom come. It doesn't help that many greens tilt left or right, or that even more greens tilt backward—away from the approach shot. The deep rough, the deep bunkers, and the monofilament fairways notwithstanding, the greens are where the Open will be won and lost. There is less truth than pathetic optimism when someone says, "The greens are holding!"

This one week in June is when the U.S.G.A. makes essentially all the money that pays for its twelve other national tournaments and for everything from its equipment-testing facilities to its museum. This has been accomplished, outside the ropes, by turning the U.S. Open Championship into a theme park with deep connotations of mall. At the western end of the course is the clubhouse, and at the eastern end—just inside the main gate—is the Merchandise Pavilion. The Open crowd is necessarily limited to thirty-five thousand people, who pay ninety-five to a hundred and forty dollars per day. A goodly number of them don't make it much past the Merchandise Pavilion, a boutique in a tent that covers thirty-six thousand square feet. It sells sweaters, vests, wind shirts, caps, jewelry, umbrellas, ball markers, balls, bags, belts—all of which bear the U.S. Open–Oakmont logo. There are more cash registers (fifty-two) than there are at L. L. Bean, and during the tournament the Merchandise Pavilion alone can take in fifteen or sixteen million dollars. Like the ancestral L. L. Bean in Freeport, Maine, the Merchandise Pavilion is now accompanied by other commercial enterprises, in smaller tents. They border a lawn where chairs and shaded tables face a two-hundred-square-foot outdoor television screen so that paying guests can watch the tournament without going on the course. The islands and aisles in the Merchandise Pavilion are studded with TV screens, too, and the place ordinarily teems with people, but when the screens show Tiger Woods going off the second tee, from which he will walk a thousand feet to the second green and the third tee—the features of the golf course that are closest to the Merchandise Pavilion—the big tent empties out as if someone had shouted "Fire!" A surge of people moves to the edge of the course for glimpses of the world's greatest golfer since Bob Jones, among them those who don't wholly believe that. After he has made his drive and gone off down the third fairway, the Merchandise Pavilion refills.

Close by is the Trophy Club, a tent in which—with an admission ticket worth a hundred and forty dollars—you can spend the day watching the tournament at a cool bar. The Trophy Club is a public version of the corporate-hospitality tents, with their decks and picket fences, which, forty-seven in all, contiguously line the edges of the course as if they were horse barns. On upholstered furniture in air-conditioned space, a guest can develop gratitude to MassMutual, Lexus, or PNC Financial Services while watching the golf on television and hearing the more than candid comments of Johnny Miller, whose 63 on this course thirty-four years ago remains the best-ever final round to win a U.S. Open Championship. The corporate-hospitality tents are rentals from the U.S.G.A. that cost as much as $175,000, not including food or drink. The I.R.S. deserves an honorary tent. When Woods goes by, the tentees step out on deck and into the heat, and line the picket fences.

The fact that some people do this is testimony to those who do not. Hardy people jam the course. The full thirty-five thousand would overload it. They are not all wearing white, but somehow collectively they turn bright white, causing the fairways to seem like streets and themselves like plowed snow. Most are in shorts, golf shirts, running shoes, and low-cut socks, and around them is an ambience of passion for the game of golf, whether they are sitting in grandstands, lining fairway ropes, speed-walking the fairway crossings, or even sleeping under peripheral trees. A high proportion are in good shape, with smooth muscular calves and flat stomachs. A high proportion, too, have glistening foreheads and bulging corporations. In ever taller stacks, they accumulate as souvenirs the U.S. Open–Oakmont-logoed containers they have emptied of beer, which they seem to drink in greater quantity than they would on couches at home.

This is an Open in which "saving a bogey" has become a mark of honor. Somebody might win that way. For the first time in thirty-three years, no player is under par after two rounds. It was thirty-three years ago that Sandy Tatum, the chairman of the U.S.G.A.'s championship committee, articulated the annual mission of the tournament, saying, "We're not trying to humiliate the best players in the world. We're simply trying to identify who they are." There is not even one hole on which this year's lineup is averaging under par. Other athletic games are played in uniform settings. In this one, the idiosyncratic course enters the competition. It seems to have no weaknesses.

Off the northeast corner of the clubhouse, an oak rises through the front row of a grandstand as if it had selected the best seat. This tree is my *querencia*. I discovered the base of it early on— after walking the course in search of vantage points, after trudging en masse with photographers trailing Tiger Woods, after lying on a knoll high above the par-3 sixth while group after group played through. The predominant sound out there is the stifled roar from invisible greens as putts lip out or stop barely shy or in various other ways come close but do not fall. Like the sound of distant bombs, these random detonations tell their stories to the golfers, some of whom are literally playing it by ear. If the roar is not stifled, it's a birdie or an eagle or a chip-in or a long putt curling home. Golfers and gallery alike, what no one is seeing on the course is most of the action. Television, for its part, sees more but is necessarily so selective that the result is a species of highlight film.

Of the on-site spectators, many elect not to move. They will choose grandstands beside greens—even back-nine greens—and fill them up solid long before the first pairing, on the first tee, tees off. In uninterrupted sun, the people in the grandstands sit patiently for several hours before the first trooping group (the golfers, the dromedary caddies, the rules official, the walking scorer, the standard-bearer straight out of the Tenth Legion holding up a placard bearing the names of the players and their current scores) appears on the fairway, approaches, arrives, chips, putts, and moves on. To shape the masses along the fairways and prevent them also from trampling the high rough (thereby creating good lies for bad shots), eight and a half miles of rope separate the public from the professional. Around my neck is a black lanyard with white block letters: "U.S.G.A. U.S. OPEN CHAMPIONSHIP." Flapping from the lanyard is a green plastic card that says "MEDIA" and "NEW YORKER MAGAZINE," and bears my face, my name, and the access code MRL (Media Center, Practice Areas, Locker Room). I was also issued an elastic armband tight enough to serve as a tourniquet. Royal blue with white block letters, it says:

INSIDE ROPES ACCESS

MUST BE VISIBLE AT ALL TIMES

MEDIA

I am wearing it around my belt, where it hangs sideways, because the photographers' armbands are all on their belts, and the style is patently cool. A few feet inside the ropes, I can go anywhere on the course, but things seem to have changed since 1950, and I'm not sure where anywhere might be. I look for clues from other people with notebooks but don't see anyone to emulate. I can walk inside the ropes where people, roped out, have been waiting six hours for a glimpse they want to remember. I not only can walk in front of them; I can stop. The protocol is to kneel or sit and not block the view. This, nonetheless, is not the most comfortable relationship I can imagine forming with these people. I once rode around the southern tip of Manhattan and partway up the East River with a rich man in his yacht. It was the Fourth of July, evening, and the public fireworks were about to begin. The public, fifty deep, lined the edge of South Street by the water. The pyrotechnics would be set off from a barge in the river. The yacht—actually, a small ship— pulled over to the South Street embankment and tied up directly in front of five thousand people. Inside the ropes at Oakmont, I'm thinking rich man's yacht. Following various golfers from tee to green, I walk alone inside the ropes, past the silent majority, feeling unloved. Sometimes I slip outside the ropes to recover my self-esteem. Following Tiger Woods is relatively painless. I just slip into the pack of photographers, and go where they go, which is always cheeky and close. After nine holes with him on Day Two, I shrugged and came back to my tree.

For a couple of hours in early afternoon, it provides some protection from the stroking sun—no small thing on a layout that has recently been denuded of five thousand trees. To elude the objections of members of the club, trees were torn out like scallions under cover of darkness and were replaced before dawn by soil and sod. Planted when the course was sixty years old, they changed its character. Henry Clay Fownes meant his Oakmont to suggest the wide-open, windswept, subtly structured links courses of Scotland—St. Andrews, Muirfield, Royal Dornoch, Carnoustie—which are on the emergent, rebounding coastline of the North Sea. That's a hard thing to bring off on the Appalachian Plateau, but Fownes did achieve at least an architectural reference, perhaps under the influence of Andrew Carnegie. Now, with so many trees gone, this scene from the oak at the clubhouse corner is unimpeded across a hundred and fifty acres of golf, half the course in one glance. From the high ground, the scene is almost aerial. The blimp overhead has a less interesting view.

This big oak, a survivor if ever there was one, is close to the eighteenth green. It is very close also to golfers and caddies on the twelfth tee, and close as well to the tenth tee. The eleventh green is just downslope. Such bunching reflects the antiquity of the course. Architects of modern layouts—mindful of, among other things, liability lawyers—place their tee boxes farther from connecting greens. When the golfers hit off on the twelfth, the crack of contact from their hydrocephalic drivers makes it seem like a rifle range. If someone happens to be putting on the eighteenth green, players on the twelfth tee go silent, hold off politely, and wait. Groups on the tenth tee do the same. The players on the tees are not only being careful not to spoil the putting but are also aware that any decent putt on the eighteenth green, let alone a great one or a great near-miss, is going to set off one of those crowd-roar bombs which could screw a drive in mid-swing.

The view from the oak, downhill over all these features, comprehends an arc of ninety degrees, from the eighteenth fairway, on the left, to the tenth fairway, on the right. It contains the whole of the back nine, and—in this uneven, periglacial topography—only a few humps and lumps hide anything. Trees line the arc beyond the bounds of play. Along the fairways, outside the ropes, people move like littoral drift around the steady populations in the grandstands. When Woods is coming through, or Phil Mickelson while he lasts, these framing galleries visibly thicken. You see them cross fairways where and when permitted, always marshalled with ropes, as intent as pilgrims on their way to Santiago. From this perspective, and in this heat, you can comprehend the dimensions and degree of difficulty not only of this course but of this game.

Because I don't know any better, and have been slow to get with it after fifty years, I have stayed under this tree for as much as seven consecutive hours while the sun turns me into beef jerky. I'm in front of the grandstand and inside the ropes, and I don't have to worry about blocking the view of anyone. The Oakmont oak is doing that for me. Sandra Day O'Connor walks in front of me, in tan slacks and a broad-brimmed hat. Photographers come and go, their numbers in direct proportion to the street recognition of the players currently on the tees or green. A long-gray-haired photographer slowly shuffles by, so laden down with dangling bags and bundles that he looks as if he sleeps in cardboard. At last—like a faint aurora over the tenth fairway—dawn comes to Rip Van Golfer. The photographers, out of absolute necessity, are out here trekking in the blistering sun. They have no alternative. There's a relative absence of notepads, because the writers are somewhere else.

When I was nine years old, a black sweater with orange stripes on the sleeves and the number 33 front and back was made for me by the same company that made the uniforms of the Princeton football team. On fall Saturdays, I ran out onto the field with them in Palmer Stadium and stood on the sidelines through the game. My father, whose practice was sports medicine before that term came into use, was their doctor. After they scored, I went behind the goalpost and caught the extra point. One miserable November afternoon, soaked in a freezing rain when I was ten, I turned around and looked up at the press box. I saw people up there with typewriters, sitting dry under a roof in what I knew to be heated space. In that precise moment, I decided to become a writer.

In the U.S.G.A.'s Media Center, I can feel again what was going on in my ten-year-old mind. The Media Center is larger than the Merchandise Pavilion. Unobtrusive, tucked away behind the clubhouse, it is the exact length of a Los Angeles–class attack submarine, and three or four times as wide. In all, the place consists of four crisply cool and contiguous tents, the largest of which contains the cable-connected desks of three hundred and fifty journalists who do not have to leave the premises to cover the U.S. Open. They see more of it if they don't. The great contemporary names in golf journalism are here: Robert Sommers, Dave Anderson, Lorne Rubenstein, Tim Rosaforte, Peter Kessler, and the rest. Damon Hack. The desk locations are loosely ranked: Associated Press, front and center; New York *Times*, Row 2; Washington *Post*, Row 3; *Sports Illustrated*, Row 4; *The Scotsman*, Row 5; *Sports Nippon*, Row 6; *Golf World*, Row 7; Sydney *Morning Herald*, Row 8; *Golf Digest* (India), Row 9. The sitting journalists, about ten per cent women, face a scoreboard a hundred feet wide that presents in real time the hole-to-hole progress of not just the leaders but every player. Flanking the board are two thirty-six-square-foot screens to which NBC and ESPN, without graphics or commentary, feed the action from outdoors. If a journalist's laptop develops technical problems, no need to call Bangalore. The U.S.G.A.'s own I.T. support staff will help. Off one end of this magnified city room is a dining area with twenty-three large round tables, on each table a rosebud *en vase*. A dozen three- and four-foot full-broadcast-television screens are arranged so that everybody at every table can see and hear Johnny Miller. In mid- to late afternoon, if action on the course becomes especially dramatic, the dining area fills up.

After players finish their rounds, some are asked to do a short press conference called a "flash interview," which takes place in an enclave outside the locker room, where the public is excluded, and fencing separates the journalists from the golfer. To leave the Media Center and participate in a flash interview, you have to get up and walk a hundred yards or so, basically around the north end of the clubhouse. Few do. It has been suggested to the U.S.G.A. that Opens be wired so that journalists can participate in flash interviews without leaving their desks, but that is not in the offing at present. Fewer than twenty do the flash interview with Aaron Baddeley, never mind that he has just finished Round 3 and leads the field by two strokes. Fewer than twenty interview Paul Casey, who shot a 60 when he was at Arizona State to break Tiger Woods' N.C.A.A. record and is now strongly threatening to outdo him here. Listening to Casey's responses to questions, a guy from *Golf Digest* is blowing bubblegum. No more than forty journalists out of three hundred and fifty come to a third-round flash with Woods himself.

If a golfer has had a particularly notable round, he is invited on to a more formal press conference in a large space in the Media Center with television cameras and folding chairs. Rand Jerris, at a table surrounded by green vegetation and adorned with enough flowers to suggest a funeral as well as a celebration, asks the first couple of questions. Then the attending press, often a group of fewer than thirty, takes over. At both forms of interview, the majority are not attending and taking notes because a court stenographer is doing it for them. With breathtaking celerity—within ten minutes—transcripts of both the flash interviews and the longer interviews are produced, reproduced, machine-stapled, never proofread, and placed in wall racks, where they are collected by the journalists. "The day will come when we e-mail interviews to them at their desks," Jerris says. If a golfer gets off a good quote—such as Angel Cabrera saying, "There are some players that have psychologists, sportologists; I smoke"—the quote is going to appear in countless newspapers and magazines as if Cabrera had whispered it into the writer's ear. Through the tournament, quotes taken by the court stenographer are repeated liberally on NBC, occasionally on simulated plaques beside pictures of the quotees.

Media Center interview two days before the tournament:

ERNIE ELS: These are the toughest greens we'll ever play in U.S. Open history, or even any other golf tournament we play.

Flash, Thursday:

Q. *How mentally tough is the grind?*
TIGER WOODS: Well, if you play most tournaments, even a major like in Augusta, even other difficult majors that we play, you probably are going to have one or two shots where you can take off, you know? It's not that hard of a shot. You can close your eyes and probably hit it either in the fairway or on the greens, it's an easy shot. On this golf course there are none, and no easy birdies, most golf courses you play, you're going to pick up a cheap birdie here and there, there are none.

Media Center, Thursday:

RAND JERRIS: We are now joined by Nick Dougherty with a round of 2-under par 68 in the first round. Maybe you could start us with some comments about your round and the playing conditions this morning.

NICK DOUGHERTY: Yeah, I think the course is—I hate saying it—easy.

Dougherty's second round will be seven over par.

Flash, Friday:

Q. *Can you talk about how you had to scramble on No. 2?*

TIGER WOODS: I tugged my tee shot left and rough snagged it coming out and the hay snagged it again. I hit a pretty good bunker shot I thought, got below the hole and made the putt, one of the very few putts where I could be aggressive. I think I had probably three putts today that I could be aggressive with and I made two of them, the rest I had to kind of feed it down there.

Flash, Friday:

Q. *No. 2 wasn't a fun hole for you; are there any there where you were having any fun at all?*

TIGER WOODS: It's so different than any other tournament we ever play in. Good shots are not going to be totally rewarded, but you're going to have good shots, bad shots are going to be penalized, and you know that and that's the way it should be, but you have to understand how to keep the ball in play, keep it below the hole if you can and have aggressive putts and I didn't do that today. Every putt seemed to be left to right, I had these feeders, I never had a putt where I felt like I could give it a pretty good rap.

Flash, Friday:

AARON BADDELEY: Like we were talking on No. 5, to get the ball like within ten, fifteen feet, you had like a three-by-three-foot landing area to land in.

Flash, Friday:

Q. How tough is a sub-par round today?
BRANDT SNEDEKER: I don't see how you could do it. It would be considered one of the best rounds of golf of the year to shoot under par. The wind is blowing so hard on some of these holes, it's virtually impossible to hit a lot of fairways. The rough is as nasty as it can be, and the greens are as firm and fast as anywhere I've ever seen. You would really have to have an unbelievably good round of ball striking and an unbelievably good round of putting to even consider breaking par out there today.

Fifteen minutes later, Paul Casey comes in in 66.

Media Center, Friday:

Q. When was the last tournament you won? . . . I know it's been a while, I don't mean to bring up a sore subject.

BUBBA WATSON: That's all right. I'm not very good. [*Laughter*]

Flash, Saturday:

Q. *Your putts were close all day; frustrating?*
TIGER WOODS: I'd be miffed with myself if I hit bad putts, but
I hit good ones, so just the way it goes. If you look back on
those putts on twelve and thirteen, filled have just carried a
little more pace; they would have been in, because they
only roll, what, six, eight inches past the hole. If they would
having a little harder, they would have been good.

Flash, Saturday:

Q: *On six, there was a photographer or someone bothering you.*
BUBBA WATSON: The media is always in your way, you know.
[*Laughter*]

The storied rivalry between Tiger Woods and Phil Mickelson
seems more intense among their fans than between the players.
The Mickelson people and the Woods people come near to being
as incurably divided as Republicans and Democrats. Now Mickelson, with a wrist inflamed since he came to Oakmont for an
early practice round, has missed the cut and departed, ruing the
liquid fertilizer and the thatched lies of a course so "dangerous"
that you could "end your career on one shot." His absence leaves
his fans in a vacuum that they are not about to fill with Tiger
Woods. They need a substitutional hero. As it happens, the two
likeliest possibilities are leading the tournament, and they tee off

together in the final pairing, Round 3. They are two of the longest hitters in the game. One of them plays left-handed, as Mickelson does, and the other looks like him. The first is Bubba Watson.

If a par 4 measures not a lot under 400 yards, Bubba can drive the green. His 460cc Grafalloy driver has a pink shaft. Its head is the size of a softball. He is six feet three and weighs a hundred and eighty pounds, and his own head is strikingly spherical. His fine black hair, projecting straight all over and mowed to six-tenths of an inch, appears to have the soft texture of an electric shoe polisher. His home town is Bagdad, Florida—population fifteen hundred, in the panhandle—where he grew up a good ol' child. His father, a onetime Green Beret who used to play golf but rarely made it into the eighties, is the only golf coach that Bubba has ever had. "He's right-handed, so we used, like, a mirror. He says I quit listening to him about age nine. You know how parents get sometimes." His father told him to hit the ball as hard as he could, adding, "We'll figure out the rest after that." When a journalist asks Bubba how difficult it is for him to forgo his passion for his driver and, in order to play it smart, wimp down to "6-irons off par-4 tees," Bubba recalls the second-round fourteenth—"358 straight downwind." He said to Teddy Scott, his caddie, "I think I should hit the driver—I can get there." Handing Bubba his 6-iron, the caddie said, "I know you can get there, but this is what we're hitting."

BUBBA WATSON: He's got a little baby, so he's got to eat, too. [*Laughter*] It's hard because it's more fun for me to hit the driver. When I'm home, that's all I hit no matter if the hole is long, short, it doesn't matter, that's all I'm hitting off tees. You look, not like a man when you're at your home course hitting iron off the tee.

In the days leading up to events on the tour, Bubba Watson and Tiger Woods frequently play practice rounds together, getting to the golf course at first light.

Media Center, Friday:

Q. *Tiger has marvelled in the past about how far you hit the ball. When you play those practice rounds with him, how far do you blast it past him, and what's his reaction?*

BUBBA WATSON: I blast by him every time. [*Laughter*] He always talks about his wins, and I always talk about how far I hit it. [*Laughter*] The man wants to hit it past everybody. Doesn't matter—you can practice and win tournaments, but you can't practice it and hit it farther, that's what I always tell him, but he doesn't listen very much. He always talks about majors and all that stuff. [*Laughter*]

Flash, Friday:

Q. *Bubba said that he bothers you asking you a lot of questions during the pre-dawn practice rounds; what is it that makes you want to keep answering him?*

TIGER WOODS: Bubba is a great kid, I enjoy playing with him and he's got so much talent and if he would just understand how to play strategically, he's got all the power, you can't teach power but you can teach strategies and he has the ability to tone it back and play different shots and if you watch him play he does play shots and he's from the old school that way, he likes to shape shots and that's a missing art nowadays.

Tiger, who is thirty-one, is three years older than the great kid. Here at the U.S. Open, to loosen up in the morning and prepare for each day's round of golf, Bubba plays basketball. Since one-on-one would be risky and in any case too strenuous, he plays Horse with Angie Watson, his wife. On one of their first dates—"the first time we hung out"—they played Around the World, a ten-shot contest from various angles on the periphery. You give up the ball when you miss. Angie hit ten straight jumpers, and Bubba never got the ball. Angie played in the W.N.B.A., for the Charlotte Sting.

Media Center, Friday:

Q. Some people might say that being a small-town guy, there's a risk of suddenly becoming wide-eyed in the final two days. Why will that not happen, do you think, being wide-eyed, realizing your a small town boy and here you are?

BUBBA WATSON: I don't know what's going to happen. I'm hopefully going to wake up in the morning and go from there. But I don't know what's going to happen. I might shoot 65-65 or 85-85. Hopefully my wife will still love me no matter what I do.

Second in the tournament by a single stroke, Bubba tees off on Saturday. If miracles could happen, he would replay the ninth.

Off the green in two, he chunks a chip (a few feet nowhere), loses his cool, loses his marbles, steps swiftly to the ball, swings without preparation, hits it over the green, chips to fifteen feet, and two-putts for a triple. "One bad swing, and that's all it takes."

Bubba Watson's playing partner is Angel Cabrera, who is very good at avoiding one bad swing, and goes on to the final round four strokes off the lead. In winning his first major, Cabrera will also become the first U.S. Open champion to speak through an interpreter. He is from Córdoba, four hundred miles northwest of Buenos Aires. Nine months older than Mickelson, three inches shorter, and ten pounds heavier, Cabrera nevertheless resembles Mickelson to an uncanny extent—in his build, in his jowly bright-eyed demeanor, and, above all, in his lumbering gait. Almost as if he is imitating Mickelson, Cabrera clomps along in a way that variously suggests a large Pleistocene mammal or a blue-collar worker on his way to fix a faucet. Cabrera is Mickelson through an interpreter, Mickelson translated into Spanish. So what if he swings right-handed? A gift to all Philistines, he's their pro-tem man.

Cabrera became a caddie at the age of ten, full time. From the primary grades, he had to drop out of school forever in order to help put food on his family's table. Caddies in Córdoba could play the course on Mondays. He was not taught; he just played—developing what has been called "a homespun swing." He became a pro when he was twenty, with the same domestic purpose he had when he became a caddie.

He smokes, yes—"*Sí, fumo*"—*cigarrillos pequeñitos*, the length of golf tees. For his manner of walking he is known in Córdoba as El Pato, the duck. His balding brush cut is graying at the temples. In the second round, on his last hole, he sank a birdie putt that caused Phil Mickelson and eighteen others to pack and go home, missing the cut. As Cabrera left the course, forty-odd journalists were doing a flash interview with Tiger Woods, a crowd that melted to fewer than twenty when Cabrera followed Tiger to do his own.

And now, through the final round, Cabrera is becoming visibly and increasingly nervous, for the simple reason that he thinks he has a chance to win. He smokes more. He smokes in several senses. He birdies the eighth. He birdies the eleventh. His drive on the long, downhill twelfth rolls out to 390 yards. After some of these shots, he claps a hand over his ball cap in amazed disbelief. After his drive on the eighteenth hole, all he needs is a 9-iron. He comes in in 69. The winner's check is $1,260,000. Defeating Tiger Woods and Jim Furyk, who are tied behind him, he is the only player in this U.S. Open to turn in two subpar rounds. His seventy-two-hole total is nonetheless five over par.

Flash:

Q. Where will the trophy go?

ANGEL CABRERA [*in Spanish*]: With me, in my bed, it's going to sleep with me. . . . It is very difficult to describe this moment. Probably tomorrow when I wake up with this trophy beside me in my bed, I will realize that I have won the U.S. Open.

In the Media Center, he responds to some of the questions without waiting for the interpreter to tell him what was asked.

Q. If you're understanding me, why aren't you answering this in English? [Laughter]

ANGEL CABRERA [*in Spanish*]: I understand, but I'm not fluent enough, so I feel that I cannot be myself.

Q. You beat the best player in the world and the rest of the field, but you also beat a very, very difficult golf course . . .

ANGEL CABRERA [*in Spanish, interrupting*]: Yes, definitely I was able to beat the best player and the best players here, but I wasn't able to beat the golf course. The golf course beat me.

NOWHERES

That August I returned to the town in New Jersey where I had been born fifty years before. It looked much the same. Any town would, after five weeks.

There was a great deal of waiting mail—08540, 08540, 08540. Not for nothing does that begin and end with a zero, I reflected. Good to be home. Nice to lift up the edges and crawl in under the only Zip Code I've ever known. A Zip that doesn't flap. A Zip that can be tied down. A Zip with grommets at either end.

I opened a letter from a staff writer at a national travel magazine compiled and edited in Tennessee.

He said, "I would appreciate it very much if you could answer some questions I have about New Jersey . . . I would like to know why a writer, who could live almost anywhere he wanted to, chooses to live in New Jersey."

Is he kidding? I have just come home from Alaska, from a long drift on the Yukon River, where, virtually under doctor's orders, I must go from time to time to recover from the sheer physiographic intensity of living in New Jersey—must go, to be reminded that there is at least one other state that is physically as varied but is sensibly spread out. New Jersey was bisected in 1664, when a boundary line was drawn from Little Egg Harbor to the Delaware River near the Water Gap so that this earth of majesty, this fortress built by Nature for herself, could be deeded by the Duke of York to Lord Berkeley and George Carteret. If you travel that line—the surveyors' pylons still stand—you traverse the physiographic provinces of New Jersey. You cross the Coastal Plain. You cross the Triassic Lowlands, a successor basin. You cross the Blue Ridge, crystalline hills. Now before you is the centerpiece of a limestone valley that runs south from New Jersey to Alabama and north from New Jersey into Canada—one valley, known to science as the Great Valley of the Appalachians and to local peoples here and there as Champlain, Shenandoah, Clinch River Valley, but in New Jersey by no special name, for in terrain so cornucopian one does not tend to notice a Shenandoah. A limestone valley is a white silo, a white barn, a sweep of ground so beautiful it should never end. You cross the broad valley. You rise now into the folded-and-faulted mountains, the eastern sinuous welt, the deformed Appalachians themselves. You are still in New Jersey.

Are they aware of this in Tennessee? When you cross New Jersey, you cover four events: the violent upheaval of two sets of mountains several hundred million years apart; and, long after all that, the creation of the Atlantic Ocean; and, more recently, the laying on of the Coastal Plain by the trowel of the mason. Do they know that in Tennessee? Tennessee is a one-event country: all you see there, east to west, are the Appalachians, slowly going away.

New Jersey has had the genius to build across its narrow center the most concentrated transportation slot in the world—with three or four railroads, seaports, highways, and an international airport all compacted in effect into a tube, a conduit, which has acquired through time an ugliness sufficient to stop a Gorgon in her tracks. Through this supersluice continuously pass hundreds of thousands of people from Nebraska, Kansas, Illinois, Iowa, Texas, Tennessee, holding their breath. They are shot like peas to New York. If New Jersey has a secret, that is it.

I remember Fred Brown, who lived in the Pine Barrens of the New Jersey Coastal Plain, remarking years ago outside his shanty, "I never been nowheres where I liked it better than I do here. I like to walk where you can walk on level ground. Outside here, if I stand still, fifteen or twenty quail, couple of coveys, will come out and go around. The gray fox don't come in no nearer than the swamp there, but I've had the coons come in here; the deer will come up. Muskrats breed right here, and otters sometimes. I was to Tennessee once. They're greedy, hungry, there, to Tennessee. They'll pretty near take the back off your hand when you lay down money. I never been nowheres I liked better than here."